The latest novel from the author of
There Must Be More To Love Than Death

Charles Newman

WHITE JAZZ

BOOKS BY CHARLES NEWMAN

    NEW AXIS   1966

    THE PROMISEKEEPER   1971

    A CHILD'S HISTORY OF AMERICA   1973

    THERE MUST BE MORE TO LOVE THAN DEATH   1976

WHITE JAZZ

CHARLES NEWMAN

The Dial Press
Doubleday & Company, Inc.
Garden City, New York
1984

for Nita, naturally enough

Library of Congress Cataloging in Publication Data
Newman, Charles Hamilton, 1938–
   White jazz.
   I. Title.
PS3564.E915W5   1984   813'.54   82-46072
ISBN: 0-385-18863-3

Copyright © 1984 by Charles Newman
All Rights Reserved
Printed in the United States of America
First Edition

Love affairs (lŭv, lŭvd, luv ĭng) *lufu, lief, ljuby.* 1. To praise; also to appraise. 2. A game of forfeits, no score for either side. 3. A small engagement, that which is done or to be done, used with intentional vagueness. 4. The benevolence attributed to God and other manifold personifications. 5. Very pleasing (applied loosely). Intransitive: to feel, frequently a vulgarism for "like." 6. Sexual passion, or, *rare*, gratification. 7. Illicit relations (obsolete). 8. A thin silky stuff, to make borders. 9. In somewhat disparaging use, amatory relations as distinguished from friendship. *Coleridge:* necessary to completeness. *Dryden:* We loved and we loved, as long as we could/Till our love was loved out in us both. *Dalrymple:* This piece is highly curious. There is no love. The whole plot is political.

Our task is to reconstruct the ship while it is floating on the ocean.

A. Einstein

Monday

During early development. the embryo consists of three hollow vesicles. triply housed and antiseptically bathed. one inside the other. On the wall that separates the two inner chambers appears a minute disc. and across it a shallow groove. the so-called primitive streak...

FROM HEAVEN it has a certain symmetry, this synapse, where the Cloverleaf appears as two pair of perfect buttocks, a cluster of genes which coyly holds the history of our future within its simple fastness. Here in four respective swales, grow four groves of twice-transplanted pin oak, the curious inflorescent leaves of which at improbable maturity, will photosynthesize all the emissions we can manage.

In this once desolate waste, beneath the buzzing arc lights, we have been brought in from the Interstate room by room, module by module, tissue and culture, discharged with the nine motels which compete within the purview of the pin oaks, and the adjacent shopping mall of salient franchises, each an infinitely expandable version of the WIDE LOAD our basic brick, measured by the eighteen-wheelers, those awesome plaques of our major arteries.

But let us travel leisurely the old peripheral roads that parallel the expressway; Frontage Road North, say, as distinguished from Frontage Road South, which parallels the opposing side of the expressway, both roads' oaks recently replaced with cyclone fencing, which serves to delimit *The Golden Age,* a columned retirement complex, about which nothing is known except that it is the object of boundless, inarticulate rage across the fence at *The Left Bank,* an upscale, vibrant young-adult community, everything a body could want: valet parking, Olympic pool, pitch 'n' putt, all-weather exercise pits, mansard-type attic *garrettes* advertising "earned autonomy."

   Sandy's studio is second tier rear, wide as two six-footers, and five six-footers long...what kind of man is it who lies exactly twice across such a room? How many such men, end to end, would it take to round the world? The window is a portrait, pleated with rubberized drapes — maples, mums, and finches aswirl — your basic astigmatic trees, flowers, birds, and a plashing streamlet...this motif carried into the bedspread and the shower curtain that shrouds the variegated onyx tub. In the commode a long illegal Monte Cristo Cuban cigar ash floats intact and expensive as a Polaris missile. Despite the air-conditioner, which perpetually micturates a visible dampness upon the wall-to-wall orange-and-yellow shag, this room is hot — sparks fly from redundant brushes of polyester at the inner thigh, the acoustical ceiling's holes seem to be growing larger and farther apart, just like the universe, the fancy expansion of which is just another misreading taken by an instrument upon a sinking platform.
   The walls are paneled in facsimile pecan; the seams like

MONDAY

those one finds, not without delight, at the insides of elbows and the backsides of knees, the stretch marks, not of birthing or a lifetime's work, but those very grooves we enter the world with, our only indication of prehistory. The walls have no give and take, they move as a muscle sheath; nothing can be extinguished here, nothing ever quite ceases. There is always *some* movement, *some* noise; the echo no doubt of that first overrated explosion...and when the air-conditioner is full on, the paneling moves apart imperceptibly, exposing between the cheap six-foot centers, and a bit of God's foam.

There is also light, of course. A cowled fluorescent above the bed, infrared in the bathroom that turns the nipples and eyelids purple as you step from the detumescent shower-spritz, one super-ceramic candlestick lamp upon the Danish combo dresser/desk. Above the octagonal onyx coffee table, a translucent globe is suspended from a chain, looped once to the ceiling, thence in increasingly less dramatic swags to its power source; all energy outlets are framed and plated with a pattern discovered in a Pompeian atrium.

Three velour Empire chairs dwarf the coffee table, the webbing of the armrests matches that of the wastebasket; and this rattan reappears cunningly about the pedestal of the TV. The nightstand has a built-in ashtray, a circle for your glass, and a groove for your pencil: this room is ready to roll....

Ah, Sandy, spread-eagled alone in bed, packaged between color-coordinated, nonallergenic ecru sheets, his parts routinely engorged, pointing at his heart....Ah, after years of roomies and relatives, Sandy has his own place now.

WHITE JAZZ

Sandy's Pontiac emerges from beneath *The Left Bank,* takes up its position in the thunder of Monday morn. Its metallic violet grows darker with the sunlight, his white whip aerial tied in a perfect reptilian arc to the bumper. The citizens band radio is off. Don't want to talk at nobody just yet. The convoy of commuters moves desultorily southward down Frontage Road North to the eight-way stoplight at the interchange.

Sandy is on his way to work at the Department of Human Resources, which work, as the indubitable crow flies, is directly across the expressway from *The Left Bank,* in the shopping mall from which the smoked-glass tower of the community college rises. From his window-at-home, Sandy can see his long impermeably sealed window-at-work, like a child's coffin in the dawn. View has always been important to Sandy, inordinately so. When he gets a raise, he will move from his *garrette* to a corner suite overlooking the entire interchange, a panoramic view of all the lights and lubricants of the wars of happiness.

He awaits the green arrow, negotiates the overpass; out here he is side by side with the old folks from *The Golden Age,* their goggled faces set upon babies' bodies, men's noses tipped in zinc oxide, ladies' lips and nails laminated with the same metallic lacquer as their cars. They have forgotten, apparently, the outline of their mouths, lost the idea of where their lips leave off, and a new mouth has been drawn in for the leisure years, slightly off center, less pursed; the philtrum filled in with epoxy. They have become ventriloquial in spite of themselves. They have begun Operation No.

As they resemble more and more a soufflé, their preference

MONDAY

for the tubular increases, the immediately graspable, the handle in the bath. Their skulls just barely clear their headrests, and suspicion and fear emanate with their no-lead exhaust. Sandy hates old folks almost as much as he hates children, which is why he lives at *The Left Bank,* where neither are permitted to abide and are barely tolerated as visitors.

Ahead of him on the overpass are teenagers packed into a sedan like some imported Balkan commodity — oiled fishsheepgoose — to be opened only with a key. They are spoiling for a fight: they give him the finger; Sandy returns it in spades. He will pull their lips over their skulls; God will drive his Peter through their brains!

Above the overpass, upon the historical grassy embankment, above a simple tomb, there is a sign erected by the Chamber of Commerce advertising the interchange:

>   FOUR WAYS TO GET ON
>   FIVE WAYS TO GET OFF

it says. Each day in the morning traffic, Sandy studies the cloverleaf, no less intently than an amateur botanist cataloguing the garden of the New World, but he has yet to discover that fifth exit. He diagrams the air with a limp index finger, but is interrupted even with the aerial down; the CB has picked up a power-boosted teamster who has just slid beneath him.

"Breaker breaker, that there purple Pontiac four-wheeler on this here bridge, you got your ears up?"

Sandy moves dutifully, hesitantly, to reply. It is a kind of vote.

"You got the Sandman, breaker, come on."

"Thanks, old buddy, just checking out my reception. How you read me?"

Sandy watches the needle of the S-meter jump.

"Just for fine, breaker. You're pushing seven pounds. What's your handle anyway?"

"This here's Maintenance Man. But I'm gone, Sandman, I got my hammer down. Maybe I'll catch you coming back, I do this trip twicet day."

"Have a good day, Maintenance Man, and a better one tomorrow."

The traffic on the overpass has broken loose, heavy motes of exhaust rise suddenly as if from a driver descending, and Sandy has the Pontiac eased into his reserved parking place behind the Department of Human Resources.

He draws his computer console across his cubicle on casters, and logs in.

The encrypted password is verified, the nonpresence of mail is announced, no message for the day is forthcoming, and, somewhat rebuked, Sandy inhibits the receipt of messages, retrieves his own file, canonicalizes his file with a reverse hire for a one-pass funding, concatenates it into a standard output, and initiates the command argument for the project-at-hand, which is finally shaping up.

MONDAY

AN ANSWER TO ALL OBJECTIONS

There is no way to tell you how sorry all of us are that you have suffered this inconvenience. We pride ourselves on the perfect condition of our products and their safety.

Unfortunately, however, the combination of man and machine is not always infallible. And with the numbers involved, there is always, statistically, the possibility of a breakdown.

Our intention, indeed our be-all and end-all, is to provide dependable quality control that merits your continued confidence, and we deeply regret hearing of incidents such as the one which you brought to our attention. Infrequent as they may be, we realize this does not make them easier to endure when one is personally involved.

Sandy is also moonlighting on his master's thesis, a cross-referenced concordance of his own personal filing cabinet. After going through *Bank, Benefits, Book Clubs, Budget, Car, Correspondence, Father, Foodstuffs, Fruit by Mail, Funny Things, Insurance, Job, Mexico, Mother,* and *Other,* he is up to *Parents* (deceased) and has *Travel* and *Vita* to go. But Sandy is always nervous the first of the week. His trachea are sticky, he is ...allergic.

"Petrochemicals perhaps, dry-cleaning fluid perhaps," his doctor says. "How could we know? There being no such thing as pure air," Dr. Onarga continues. "We eliminate the variables one by one, and if they are isolatable, you will be desensitized. Once nature is mastered, you see" — he winks — "she no longer behaves as she once did, i.e., regularly." Dr. Onarga is a holistic periodontist with a secondary specialty in allergy/addiction. "You cannot treat bleeding gums as an isolated pathology, you must take the totality of the patient and his environment into account. Plaque is the sign of a diseased spirit."

Dr. Onarga has four offices at four different interchanges along the Interstate, spending one day in each. Each office is manned by four attractive girls, doubling as para-periodontists, ancillary allergatrixes, all in white, disciples of a sort; white dresses, white stockings, and clean sharpened genitals. They make up the serums, illustrate the plaque, give the injections, issue directions for detoxification, for flossing, and make you pay.

"Sure I'm a Gypsy," Dr. Onarga admits. "And, it's true, you know. Maybe we'll never find out what's wrong with you."

When Onarga took Sandy's case history he dismissed any family-related diseases. "What we're after, Mr. Sandman, is the new expression of preexisting genes. To survive, in your state, it will be necessary to produce new ethers. Will nor hope nor history will avail. We are dealing with genes that have been, well, *mushed*... and surface randomly in hybrids like yourself. Your space is a web of many overlapping vibratory emanations. They may be too much for you, but there is no escaping them. You must become a healer to yourself, and a healer is one who can

MONDAY

transmit the highest frequency manageably. You must learn to neutralize yourself. Cultivate the steady state. I suspect electromagnetic unsympathies. We'll know more when the results of your atomic testing are in..."

Today Sandy is leaving out salts and frozen things. Yet the headaches persist. They are localized and constant. They appear to be unrelated to stress. At 10:48 A.M. the Sandman develops an egregious ongoing erection. Ten more hours until *El Cielito Lindo* opens!

> We wish to assure you that the matter has been brought to the attention of the representative in charge of your area so that any recurrence may be prevented.
> If you have occasion to use our product again, please give us another chance! We *hate* unnecessary problems as much as you do.

The Humanist busywork persists until lunch. In the lunch line he keeps one hand in his pocket to disguise the adventitious dream of *El Cielito Lindo*.

El Cielito Lindo is located in The Breakers Motel and no one knows who owns The Breakers Motel except that the same architect who did *The Left Bank, The Golden Age,* and Dr. Onarga's offices also did The Breakers Motel, whose lounge is far and away the most profitable enterprise amongst her eight sister motels in the interchange; nothing finer, nothing finer at all than to spend a few hours in *El Cielito Lindo* each evening. The lounge is always filled to capacity; salesmen fight viciously to be transferred within its territory, to be transported, transformed.

At four-fifteen Sandy is out early, on the overpass, and the aerial, like his parts, is no longer attached to the bumper.

"Hey, there, big old purple four-wheeler on that bridge! You got a Smokey report for me?"

"Haven't heard nothin' myself."

"You gettin' on? I'll watch your front door, heh."

"I'm crossing over, good buddy, we'll see you one day."

Arriving at *The Left Bank,* Sandy goes poolside for his daily fifty laps to relieve the swollen pupace, laid along the inner seam of his tank suit, as always pointing in the direction that he is going. Sheila, the para-legal, giggles into a rum and coke as Sandy sidestrokes; the cusps of her muff protrude from her short shorts.

The Sandman removes himself to the sauna where the redundant *oom*pah may be sweated out, the whites of his large blue eyes now stained a cloister red from the chlorine.

Then out of those flared slacks and wide tie into the navy turtleneck and crotch-respecting jeans for dinner while the new TV serial blares its relaxing continuity, voice over.

"The Great White Horse, was originally one of four who spent all their time grazing about the heavens. Once, however, a malevolent God sent a storm through the air. None of the horses

MONDAY

had ever seen or heard of a storm, so they were not sufficiently wary of it. They had never been very wary. They had only seen sunlight, stars, and moonlight, and an occasional comet. They knew no fear. Thus, when the storm came up about them, they were all destroyed, dashed from heaven to earth. However, a benevolent God noticed this unfortunate situation and plotted to amend it. From the bodies of the original four, he was able to fashion a single new horse, white like the others and just as much of a flyer. There were several differences with this one, however. For example, he was able to come to earth on his own, slowing his reentry by means of a parachutelike tail and mane. He also had a considerable and sophisticated sense of fear. He was very, very wary. And not without cunning. His reproductive ability was most unusual. He was unable to give rise to a horse. But he could impregnate any type of animal, bird, or fish as he chose — within reason, of course. So that a shark might give rise to a bass, and an eagle give rise to a mockingbird. A horse might give birth to a deer, and a giraffe a small bear or cow. And thus the earth was populated. But even with these many variations, he soon became weary and bored, longing for someone to ride with! With this in mind, he set out to create for himself a companion. He searched for a beautiful woman, with the intention that she produce a man he could carry on his back, so neither would ever be alone again on heaven or earth. Such a woman he found and this he did. However, to his considerable surprise, the woman died in childbirth, and instead of giving rise to a child, gave rise to a fully developed private investigator...."

Ah, dinner, dinnertime.

WHITE JAZZ

In the mornings, *The Left Bank* is an axe blade wedged in the prairie, but in the evenings, it becomes an ocean liner, the windows fork over their opacity, every window in the world is interesting at night, the opalescent warmth is overwhelming, the building becomes an enormous readout panel, comforting gauges of the cockpit, all information at your fingertips, and what's more, it obligingly *stays* at your fingertips, as the command module is scanned for the single roseate blinking bulb that isolates malfunction and cries out for correction. Sometimes, after making sure he is alone, Sandy hugs the corner of the building, his cheek against the cool strip of anodized aluminum, he can feel the reliable buzz of life, the moans of closed heat machinery....

The traffic loosens, the pavement smooths, the overpass vibrates as if it were suspended from the stars. Once over the bridge the pavement becomes viscous, all that piss and vinegar leaking into it all day, the asphalt is shredded head lettuce, the Pontiac pickled cabbage.

In *Bruno's* pizzeria the waitress is nice enough; the garbanzos are crunchy, the croutons are crunchy, the celery sticks are very crunchy, but across the small pond of his beer, Sandy spies the thick-armed counterman take down a five-gallon can of dehydrated onions and pour a bucket of water into them. The girl takes his order, "a fifteen-incher with everything." Then, as his pizza is slipped into the oven, Sandy slips out into the night; this will keep them on their goddamn toes! Pizza with Everything for Nobody!

MONDAY

He retreats to *Pauline's*, where he orders the standby, a Polish with jalapenos to go. It appears from a small, screened window which is immediately slammed. The Smokies watch Sandy eat from their patrol car, wide-brimmed hats pulled tightly over their thick brows, checking the alignment of Sandy's bite, a corrected chomp achieved over a period of four adolescent years at a cost of nearly $11,000. Reflect on that, porker and peppers, as the bun is forced upward past the pointed incisors into the upper palate. At twenty-five, Sandy is beginning to develop a healthy respect for reticence.

Gazing at the Smokies, his mouth full, Sandy is aware of irrational team allegiances, and he has made it a moral point that the internal rhythms of whatever game he is watching never become his own. He eschews the dangerous precedent of "the season"; he watches baseball only during the Series, and then only if it goes to games six and seven; only the fourth quarter of the crucial game four of the home and home basketball play-offs; and as for football, only the instant replays at halftime in the last half of the season before the play-offs, when betting and theory both peak. Sandy admires selectivity more than anything.

"You don't have to watch anything close anymore," he tells Dr. Onarga, at one appointment, "'cause it'll always be repeated." Dr. Onarga nods and hums a Gypsy lullaby. Through the opaque X-ray illuminator, his gaze is fixed beyond the Carpathians to the East, the East of the Trading Routes, the turreted impregnable towns at the crossroads, where all secondary cultural characteristics are suspended in the minting of hard currency.

Back in his *garrette* with only two more hours till opening, he works his CB base station on the wicker trunk at the foot of the bed. Above the bed, thumbtacked to the Spanish-type headboard, are two Polaroid photos...Tyler and Travis, his dead parents. Sandy took the pictures a few years back, and the once nearly fluorescent colors have faded. They are standing on a dock. A lake spreads out behind them. They are wind-tanned. The wind is blowing in their brittle hair. They wear matching sweat shirts with the lake's name on them. It is a fine sharp fall day. There is a mess of fish in a corner in the picture. Lake trout. Great northern. Ohhhhhhhhhh. He experiences an Xanthein rush. He holds himself.

The wiring for the base station has been completed. Sandy has a new crystal in a jeweler's vise; with a diamond cutter he makes a groove, a streak, its clean fresh dust immediately absorbed into the room's normal banal dust. Between the factory marks, through a thick lens, the Sandman cuts the groove for a new channel exactly between the government/military and citizens bands — 27.407 megahertz. At first there is discernible silence, then some primordial formulaeic static. Then static in a siren pattern. If not contact exactly, continuity. The oldest echo. The sirens of incredulity. He has divided static from silence and the static is good.

"Breaker, breaker," Sandy intones. "This is the Sandman. Anybody out there, heh? Anybody got their ears up?"

Comforting static ensues. Only a matter of time before a new quandary will be bridged. The digital campanile of the community college bongs out ten strokes.

MONDAY

Sandy removes his jeans — the one rule at *El Cielito Lindo* is *no denim* — slips into his beltless cuffless pocketless cowboy twill slacks with the eight-button fly, the striped V-cut Thundershorts, the Mexican wedding shirt cut deep at the throat, an intricate series of flaps, pleats, and ruffles, brushes his teeth carefully, after Onarga's disclosing agent has revealed the plaque, seals his armpits, winds the gold chain twice about his neck, slips into the angora socks with the dancing pads, and the magenta penny loafers, the hue of state police cars.

The Pontiac nudges into one of the few spots left at The Breakers. Above him, two hundred feet in the air, the marquee revolves; no ballyhoo here, just

CIELITO LINDO LOUNGE DANCE

in bold type to attract the barefaced italic bedfellows.

The lobby had been recently redecorated; the predominantly Spanish motif modified. Above the gas logs is a portrait of a man reading in a leather easy chair before a fire, a brace of setters at his feet. The walls and trim have a revolutionary cast; Valley Forge green, Minute Man blue, Colony red, and Springfield Rifle gray.

On the double glass doors of The Breakers a "No Vacancy" sign sways as if lacking certitude. In the lobby a man is belaboring a bank of phones concerning an aborted rent-a-car agreement in Cincinnati two days before.

A nuclear family of six has been caught innocently in the action. Mom is splayed with the unfed youngest in a paislied wing chair, Dad's tummy conforms gelatinously to the molding of the front desk, the eleven-year-old girl trembles thin as an alder in the dark vestibule of vending machines and video games, while seven-year-old boy-twins push obsolescent styrene autos about the long bladed feet of two cocained Cubans, who are only slightly less revulsed by this spectacle than Sandy himself. The autos stall in the heavy shag, the Cubans salute desultorily, and only a dozen feet away from the entrance to the lounge issues the *El Cielito Lindo* theme song.

Ay yi, yi-yi
Come to your window

Sandy skirts the pride of Cubans who have repaired to a circular red-plush banquette where they cross and cross their bandy legs. They are waiting for the lounge to overflow, the periphery to coalesce, break away as algae on a stream; they will pick off the stragglers and inoculate them.

Strictly Amateur Evening so far: milling swilling yahoos, dumb cunts, poor fuckers, the Skanks who never scare, the Nerds who never score. The Skanks, hairpieces piled on their thin skull plates, they are so demanding, the Skanks, and yet they seem to get so very little for their efforts, the Skanks. What happens to such egregious ongoing unsatisfied demand? Does it rise into the ozone and acidify the rain? Some evenings it seems almost palpable, impacted like old chewing gum against the ceiling, aerosoling in the corners. It hovers, melds with dust; it cannot rise despite its lightness; is it possible that such demand is what Sandy is allergic to?

MONDAY

Of the Nerds, let us not judge. Their lot is the more hopeless, since they cannot blame their lack of success on looks or money; style is their downfall. Many a Nerd has made it through sheer willfulness; the entire world is their exhibition, they succeed in spite of themselves, and if we are not amused, we nevertheless make way for them.

The Skanks do not believe in luck, though perhaps increasingly in collective will. But whereas the Nerds must actually produce power, the Skanks must not only transmit information, they must maintain a *state,* until an effective procedure is plugged in. Then the rules change, and they enter *another state;* they make the transition if they care to, and mostly they do. If it sounds easy to maintain a *state,* this is a great misconception, one whose debt is only now being amortized. It is said that the Skanks are capable of an *astronomical* number of *states.*

Over in the serving bar, Sandy can make out the ovulate buttocks of Wanda June, roll girl by day, queen of the *Lindo* barmaids by night; she spies Sandy and brings him a tinkling scotch, not the bar scotch but Johnny Walker, laughing in a nice imitation of anticipation. An ounce of justice has been meted out and the litigation has begun.

Sandy's scotch is inverted, and the transparent shields, one on his chest, one in his ass, begin to lose their muscilage. His lungs are rescored. He reaches down through his elastic waistband, through the striped Thunder-shorts, and massages a whorl of hair. He walks the long bar, not recognizing a single expectant face, slack jaws hung with tendril and vine. On the very last stool a dull knife of a woman in a red gown is crooning:

WHITE JAZZ

> *Oh Johnny Walker*
> *I love you*
> *I'll fuck you*
> *But every time you put me down*
> *You put me on the floor*

Sandy's shields fall with a clatter. At the inner circle, in the cockpit below the stage, the bestest baddest dancers always sit at the tiniest tables, athletic professionals awaiting the unsingable national anthem. An outer ring of tables-for-four forms the second tier, each with a plastic candle bowl, illumined fishnets encased in amber; the netting projects a webbing across the faces... everyone has been scarred in exactly the same way.

And here comes the band! *Ruby, Nimrod, and the Conquerors of Babylon:* big-lipped drummer, two poker-faced guitarists, and one solemn fellow who does nothing but diddle with the amplifiers, Maestro Luncheon. As for Nimrod, we are glad that he is employed, that he is heavily taxed for both his pleasure and his profession. Of Ruby we can say only her fine throat and navel compensate for her nasal; her charisma lies in her knowledge that her appeal is lodged in our mind's eye; nothing she could ever do will ever mitigate her charm. Charm can get you anything, Sandy knows, anything except competence. Yet even Ruby could prove to be a disappointment. Yes, no *one* person can satisfy you in *El Cielito Lindo;* nobody here says you're wrong and I'm right!

Sandy is a touch melancholy, for when his shields clatter to the carpet no one is aware. He sidles up to a loudspeaker and

MONDAY

cocks his head against the vibrating cloth, all ears. He is filled with the beat, the base line enters every orifice; melody has no place here. But as his body is filled, adumbrated, Sandy realizes there is nothing, nothing coming out of Sandy.

He breaks with the sound. The dancing has become wilder. Nimrod raises two fingers in the Victory sign for the *El Cielito Lindo Stomp,* in which your instep is knocked gently against your partner's, then shin to back of knee, and, penultimately, the flat of the ankle to ass...WHOA. the evening's mission has announced itself. Two large early thirties Art Deco married ladies on their night out, big as life, taking their slumming very seriously indeed. At home on Sandy's TV, four detective series are resolving themselves simultaneously: gun battles beneath a hydroelectric project, on top of an unfinished skyscraper, in a warehouse, down in a sewer.

Sandy grabs Wanda June, sets her tray of drinks on the lap of an astonished cowboy-looking fellah, pulls her to the perimeter of the flail and stomp, and, tucking in his shirt, does it halftime, in syncopation...the ladies club's eyes are upon him. His joints pop like flounder dropped into the hold. Inurgently, the passional auditing is peaking; Operation and/or has begun.

These are really big ladies, six-foot mothers! One in a below-the-knee pink riding skirt and flowered halter, seashell necklace, bracelets of tortoise, a blond racing stripe across her bangs; the other one, prettier possibly, in open-toed pumps, sleeveless tricot blouse, Gucci scarf, a bit of macramé here and there, and a nice mandala of bewildered earnestness in the middle of her face.

Wanda June kicks a toe above the Sandman's brow; he snaps his thickening fingers. *The Conquerors* have taken a break, but the tape of their newest album takes right over, *Words of Life on the Wings of Melody*. Sandy bites Wanda June's wet nape; a true hellion of a kiss that melts the forest of eyes at the bar.

The salesmen have arrived in their dramaturgical double knits. One stands out, a leader in some larger town, handsome silvery-haired gray-and-white-striped double-breasted seersucker, every inch an officer, here on some mysterious territorial debriefing. Sandy breaks from his slight despond; he simply cannot believe his luck. God had provided him with a stalking horse! The handsome gentleman is now bending between and courting the two ladies. Don't be a pig, hey, Mr. Vice-President of Internal Operations! She of the riding habit responds with alacrity, but she of the macramé looks straight ahead of her into the space where Sandy was dancing. The mandala has become a gear! A predestined slow mood-piece comes on and our executive has the haltered lady out on the floor. They are dancing on their toes!

Sandy takes over the dancing lady's empty chair, appropriates her *El Cielito Lindo* doily. In a silent toast his scotch displaces his new companion's face. She aligns the stem of her whiskey sour with his nose. He is careful to say nothing that might deny him the votes of the large industrial states. In the lovely unspokenness, the undancing lady loosens the chin strap on her sunbonnet. Sandy very nearly exclaims but bites his tongue.

Sandy mulls the meaning, the options here. Either she wants

him or she doesn't. This is a problem, a world in which there is no difference between dancing and fucking, everyone moving about in a slow, lilting semiotic fückstrot.

They are speaking now, Sandy and the pretty lady, but it's not at all clear who's saying what in all the din except it turns out the dancing lady is not her friend at all. Wanda June has brought two more drinks, but then she always does. It's apparent, however, from their expressions and unhurried gestures, that this is no impromptu routine, no crass negotiation. All conversation in *El Cielito Lindo* is charged with infinite innuendo, a common purpose, a single people with one language and one unmistakable meaning; no division, no confusion here, they will treat one another as equals and show mutual respect and dignity without old-fashioned reserve or role playing, conversation between consensual adults, straight talk.

"My dad," Sandy reminisces, "used to say that to be really free, to be successful in your beingness, is like being a good hitter. Everyone wants to be free, everybody wants to play every day, but there's no way if you can't hit, no matter how well you field, no matter how much spirit you have, no matter how you master the little things, the intangibles, no matter how great your attitudes, the unselfishness that makes a winner, you'll play just as long until they bring up a real hitter — then you'll be on the bench and the bench is no place for a free man. But nobody, see, knows what makes a hitter; hitting can't be taught; the best hitters can't even tell you how they do it. Oh, sure, they say things like *be free up there*, but they can say *that* to you on the bench, *be a free swinger up there*, they say, but most great hitters are lousy coaches and even a great hitter is still guessing up there, even the *best* Punch and Judy hitter is not a free swinger, he can't afford to guess. To be a real hitter you have to be smart enough to take a pitch or two, I guess...."

"*My* dad was into fishing," she eagerly rejoins. "The only bamboo that was good enough for him was a special one that came from a tiny province in China, Kwang-si; Tonkin cane he used to call it, honey, Tonkin cane, *Arundinaria amabilis,* he used to say, honey, isn't that pretty, honey, *Arundinaria amabilis?* It's the cellular structure of the cane that gives it elasticity and resistance to fatigue, all the subtle requirements that you might expect in a fine rod. You might just know that all female bamboos flower only *once* every thirty to one hundred years, depending on the species; and when this particular species flowers in Kwang-si, its near relatives flower all over the world at the same time, and after they all flower, they die; they go to seed, so to speak, all at the same time, and this causes great hardship not only to anglers, but whole communities in Asia are virtually wiped out, and they have outbreaks of bubonic plague. Rats really go for female bamboo that's gone to seed...."

"You're my quarterback," Sandy interrupts.

She is scanning him like an air comptroller, head lowered, neck sunk down in the collarbone, resisting the impulse to ignore the *blipity-blip* in the central nervous system's radarscope and gaze down the long ribbon of landing lights, those lights which somehow serve only to make everything darker. Sandy has wings over his eyes, and a small pair over his heart, a pelican's pair on his haunches, wings everywhere except where they should be.

MONDAY

Then all the pairs of wings go rigid; they are ailerons, brakes. The nacelles of the engines flare orange. The lady's thumbs are up, he has asked for and received clearance, she checks her chronometer — such a large watch for such a little wrist — and then they are arm and arm in the lobby, a matched pair of high-stepping trotters, hauling a driverless sleigh filled with unlabeled but beautifully wrapped packages to be opened one by one. It is not difficult to resist degradation in the lobby — the mauve couple in the corner, for example, with their hands thrust up one another, and the Cubans with their hypodermic dicks.

She opens her own door, on a room very much like Sandy's, formed to be inhabited, very much like the other three hundred and sixty-odd in The Breakers, as wide and clean as an express lane. The mist from her recent bath condenses upon the windows, the mirrors turn opaque; she nevertheless draws the drapes and they are surrounded on all sides by modular panels of maples, mums, and finches, trees, flowers, and the plashing streamlet, the scene replicated every six feet, lying naked now arm in arm, repeating now what will be repeated eventually in every room about them, just as the trees and flowers and plashing streamlet repeat about them, in the evening of their day; each day a thousand years....

At the chimera of midnight the waters have been divided from the waters — all is lubricious; there are waters everywhere; the fundament has appeared beneath the firmament. Rivulets of saliva, perspiration cascade down the inner creases, the seams we have spoken of, commingle in inexplicable declivities; sternum, the fault between the stomach muscles, everything slips effortlessly, huge slabs of cordwood, barked and split, shine around their sawmill; once cured, they will be lathed into Mediterranean-type TV pedestals, lathered with polyurethane gloss, but for now the wood gleams and soaks in its resin, the grain has been exposed to the elements, and it marbles spectacularly in their daze.

She leaves a tousled, crumpled Sandman and prepares a second bath, squatting in a rectangle of pure air. The lady, however, has mistaken exhaustion for morning, which at The Breakers does not begin until noon, when the inventory is taken and the cash flow reaffirmed. She has confused the ocean with the solid crystalline sphere of sky. She balls her tiny fists, stretches her arms, and her breasts pull not quite flat. Sandy knows the phone when he hears it. As it quit, the red message light pierced the dark like Mars itself.

About the only unattractive thing about Corrinne L. Huff was her laugh, or rather its silence. The jubilation of her adolescence had been so unabashed and full-throated, and her parents and peers had teased her about it so severely, that she had taken to arresting mirth by opening her mouth so theatrically wide as to cut off the epiglottis, and it was this noiseless image of a guffaw, a lovely sketch of a laugh, which now spent itself upon Sandy's clear brow.

He had entered the bath from the mirrored door, a fifth of Johnny Walker in hand, and, bending from the waist, like a good unpompous maître d', kissed the dark and massy islet rising from the water. When she laughed, he sat back startled on the closed commode.

"Why are we so good together, Sandy? Just because we're new to each other?"

"Because we've got nothing to prove?" Sandy offered, staring at the blinking message light on the extension phone.

"It's odd you should say that. It's just lately that I've wanted to prove something."

"With me?" Sandy said nervously.

"Not exactly...just with everybody," she said very softly.

Sandy seemed distracted. He sat on the edge of the commode, elbows on knees, rubbing his eyes. Then her buttocks were on his knees' red spots his elbows had left. Sandy steadied himself on his palms, blowing her hair aside so he could watch the message light. He never could let a phone ring.

"You know," she said from over his shoulder, "from the back you don't look more than fifteen."

"It's a bad back, though. Inside, I mean. I have to sit down to urinate now."

"This is not a problem..." she began argumentatively, but the phone now rang again sharply, and her hands went to her heart. Sandy picked up the bath extension without a word as she dried herself furiously.

"Mommy," the phone crackled, burned in the Sandman's hand. "Mommy!"

She snatched the receiver from him. "Oh Christ, Brucie, what's wrong?"

"When are you coming home, Mommy?"

"Tomorrow, honey, just like I told you."

"Well...uh," a deeper voice broke in. "Nothing's wrong here, dear. We just wanted to call before bed. I didn't see the harm..."

"Christ, it's after midnight, Fred! That child has school."

"It's only ten here."

"Get your goddamn time zones straight, Fred!"

Water streamed from Corrinne's eyes.

"All right, Brucie?" Fred said. "See, Mommy's all right."

"Mommy's just fine, Brucie. You bless Mommy in your prayers, hear?"

"Bye-bye, Mommy. I miss you."

"Of course you do. Give Daddy a big kiss." She replaced the receiver gingerly.

Sandy was smoking a small cigar.

"How's everything at home?"

"Fine, to hear them tell it."

"Is what you're trying to prove, have to do with him?"

"Not exactly."

"Sounds like a nice family."

"Of course. I have a talent that way too."

"I don't have a family."

"You don't seem like the type, if I may say so."

"As a matter of fact, I don't have anyone. And you know what?"

"What?"

"It doesn't seem to make a bit of difference."

MONDAY

"Of course."

"Of course what?"

"Just...you know."

"Yes, well of course I'd like to have one, a family, some day."

"Course."

"Course...I guess you don't want to talk."

"Dammit," the lady yelled, pounding her thighs, Sandy dropping ashes over his chest and then flailing madly at the sparks, "goddamn you, don't you know what's happening with *women?*"

Sandy looked around for an ashtray, both hands cupped with ashes. His chest was smeared with charcoal, his parts become quite small.

"You mean...women...in general?"

"If you like. In America for starters."

"You mean they're more...outgoing...and all?"

"Go on."

"No, I don't know much about it, I guess. It's a lot easier to get laid, acourse."

"So *that's* how you think about it."

"Look, lady, were you saving this number for *me?*"

"You appear to be a sane, strong, and decent young man who ought to know better. Who ought to know what's coming off!"

"Know what?" Sandy had reflexively slipped on his Thunder-shorts.

"Don't you ever talk about this with your girl friends?"

"What business is it of mine…?"
"They don't tell you what it's *like* to be a woman?"
"They don't complain much, if that's what you mean."
"They have their life and you have yours. Is that…*it?*"
"Well I wouldn't say that, exactly."
"And I suppose I'm the exception that proves the rule."
"Which rule?"
"Kiddo, don't you believe there're some things people can't express, but still they can feel them happening all around them? That we're on the edge of things?"
"Personally or politically?"
"In-between."
"And down the road?"
"You're not going to like it."
"I'm not liking it right now much, ma'am."
"Well, put it this way. Why were you attracted to me?"

Sandy thought for a while, his clear brow knotted like an intestine and, as if it were a prerequisite for reflection, he slipped on his slacks and socks.

"Well, lady, you're smart, and pretty enough, but maybe what I like best about you is the way your ass is connected to your brain."

"*Very* disarming," she said desperately.

"Hey, let's go get some dinner. Be civilized."

"What's civilized about dinner?"

"O.K., let's have something sent up."

"I'm not hungry, and that's it, sonny, that's what's happening."

Sandy paused respectfully. "I don't think that's what you meant to say."

She lay back and, wrapping an ice cube from her drink in a washcloth, laid it upon her sinuses.

"You know, lady, I just don't get it. If you just could say what you wanted, you'd probably get it."

"How could *you* know what *I* want?"

"That's what I just said."

"Look, sonny, I simply can't decide whether I want to throw off everything inessential or get more of everything. Can't you understand?"

"Oh, *lady,* that's just how a man feels."

"Go get something to eat yourself. Go home. I've got to beat this cold before I leave tomorrow."

"You want me to come back later? I can do it."

"Suit yourself."

"I will *not*," Sandy said with some dignity, "take the onus for this snafu!"

"You know, sonny, you are beginning to smell like my husband."

"Oh?"

"Yeah. Scotch."

Sandy thought for a moment as he slipped on his shirt.

"Well, then," he said, "you smell like your husband too."

Then he left without another word, for some reason carrying his loafers on his two longest fingers like a part-time fisherman with two incredulous champion trout. As he shut the door softly, he heard the woman who thought like a man begin to cry.

She woke hearing moans. She reached out to embrace Sandy but found only slick sheet. Then she thought she was dreaming, not awake in a strange town; her own difficult breathing had startled her, and this was somehow indicative of her life, forever being shaken out of real release, prevented from dreaming by her own banal breath. But slowly the inventory of the room took stock of her; the dumb mums and lousy finches, the stiff vinyl drapes, the emphysemic whine of the air conditioning enforced themselves. The moans reached a crescendo. A woman's moans, and not three feet from her through the wall — that conventionally rhythmic cry, somewhere between ecstasy and pain, a wordlessness refined to the point where it could be taken in whatever way its interpreter wished, named by every man to suit his fashion. It was the first time she had heard it from another, and she lay rigid, nearly comatose, waiting anxiously for the silences to come.

Then she was in her robe in the hall, standing before the adjacent room where moaning had given way to the laconic low squabble of late-night detectives. She was startled by a stunning black maid in a pinafore, at least six feet two with the face of a West Indian goddess, who strode peremptorily down the hall and disappeared through double swinging doors into the Help's respite room. She watched the doors until they ceased shuffling

MONDAY

against one another, and then she heard voices again, charmingly accented, then tearful, and finally sobbing. From behind every door, the women whispering, sighing, weeping.

Back in her room, she bolted the door, then unlocked it, realizing Sandy would misinterpret if he chose to return. At 3 A.M. she turned on the TV and spun the dial—Charlton Heston, Jesus!—snapped it off; then, her lungs crackling with dehydration, she tried to open the window, but it was sealed. She filled a water tumbler with the last of the scotch, and began to count the finches. There were 247 fucking finches in the room. She tried the lyre-back chair at the writing desk; under the glass top a card garlanded with puppies and rhododendrons announced: We shall do our utmost to please you. Above the desk, she reached for a book but found that the spines of the leather editions had been sawed off and glued to a board. And then in the mirror she caught sight of her damaged bed, the pillows and sheets scattered about the floor, exploded as artificially as in a store-window display, a buyer's market...then she dialed long distance. But when Fred's cloudy voice, circumspect even in sleep, answered, she banged the receiver down and felt, for the first time in her thirty-odd years, that she was perfectly capable of both inconsequence and betrayal.

Now it *was* dawn. She sat cross-legged in her chair, eyeing herself in the mirror in a way that she hadn't since her teens. She opened her robe slowly, then let it fall back. She touched her stomach, ran her hands over her crispness, as if it were a stranger's pet, and then lay back, strangely calm. She had come to that irrefragably momentous American knowledge; she was, in the most complex way, simply fed up. She didn't want to go home. She didn't want to stay away and live it up. She didn't want to apologize to Sandy; she didn't care if she saw him again but knew she would. She didn't want to take the night flight to Acapulco, she didn't want to buy one more single thing, she wanted her husband and her son in the worst way, but not the way they were; she didn't want to be anybody else, or with anybody else, and she didn't want to be alone. She knew that no person, no feeling, no idea would ever solve the common problem of this slightly overheated, overdecorated room. The abiding question of self-esteem seemed, if topical, nevertheless out of order.

She put the night latch on the door, confirmed her plane reservations, left a heavy tip for the mysterious beautiful maid, and after a heavy dose of antihistamine and the last of Sandy's scotch, watched the room close about her, a foot at each blink.

In the air again. The plane follows the expressway in its huffy ascension. She can differentiate *her* interchange only by the glass tower of the community college and the *El Cielito Lindo* painted in orange letters on a helipad on The Breakers' roof. It had never occurred to her before that a plane could make a shadow.

We are patient, relaxed, only at incredible speeds. It is only then, when there is no wheel to grab, no pedal to push, that our fatalism is wholly convincing. Pale, without makeup, hair tied severely back, on the aisle this time, Corrinne has requested the bulkhead seat facing the galley. Beyond, the cockpit's closeted controls. Each time the stewardess passes, her elbow brushes her hair, and, with a couple of bloody marys under her belt, this is all right. Everyone on the flight is drunk.

She is wedged in among the conventioneers, fedoras still high on their foreheads, sweating even at 32,000 feet, like the one pecan in the packet of cashews just handed her labeled "mixed nuts."

The men all have on heavy college rings, wedding bands, and nameplates: Harold, Dick, and Fitz. She has the same, except hers are a bit smaller. In fact, everybody on the entire plane seems to have on rings and nameplates, from the Jewish rear stewardess, T. Rich, to the imperturbable Scandinavian Captain Anderson. The men are talking a highly technical language, perhaps out of some long-forgotten embarrassment. They are not your everyday salesmen, but some kind of engineers, probably petrochemicals or geomorphological. She winces out of the window. The landscape below the light cirrus appears to be a load of soiled diapers. The men are elbowing each other, fighting for breathing room; they are talking about getting mugged; the windows are steaming up. Somebody says, "Well, what the hell do they expect me to do? Start over at forty-two?" She wishes her laugh was not soundless. She would like the sound, not just the shape, of her laugh back, please.

Somebody has left the cockpit door open; the navigator is reclining and reading a comic book, welded in the curve of his brown hands. The pilot and copilots' heads are bathed in the Caribbean light of their incredible instrumentation. A tight-lipped woman emerges from the forward toilet. Her eyes are also red and wet. Garbage is mounting about them: discarded newspapers, cups and napkins, gutted mixed-nut sacks, so many different kinds of tissue. The cold has gone to her chest. 'Why do they give you a menu when there's no choice,' she thinks. 'Why do they build the shore so close to the sea? How high do you have to fly before you cast no shadow?'

The man next to her is singing to himself. When their elbows brush, he jerks an unspoken, involuntary apology. She has no more questions, so she watches the stews. In the island of the lavatory, they exchange their pumps for flats, their slacks for culottes, their jackets for blouses and apronettes. Their epaulets and braid are piled in the corner with sanitary napkins and airsickness bags. They slam everything, even the tiniest doors in the galley. All the little doors and windows have made them crass. Girls without grace, but this is impossible between takeoff and landing, a good plane with no blood on it. The intercom has been found defective. The primary stew coils the microphone's impotence about her wrist, grinding her teeth. Another holds the yellow scrotum of an oxygen bag above her head, blowing on a tube, while yet another reads the prepared text as best she can without amplification. She knows no one can see her and certainly no one listens to her, even in three languages, except perhaps one random disguised inspector. To their everlasting credit, they are laughing at themselves. The eggs are under radar, the baby's milk is being boiled. Shit, they say. Another baby. The champagne has been broken out. And the clouds, the cirrus, are becoming themselves as we cannot.

MONDAY

Corrinne has resolved to worry no more — about herself, at any rate — and releases her seatback. But as she does so, a strange and constant pressure exerts itself upon her kidneys. She glances over her shoulder and sees a little boy behind her, clutching his mother's wrist, his legs stiffened in fear against her seatback. The woman is about her age, but puffier and paler; nothing, clearly, but a mother. But then she hears her own voice, if not exactly her choice of words, as well as that of Brucie...and them all.

"Don't kick the seat. Didn't you see that lady turn around?"

"I'm scared, Mama."

"Look. Here're the directions. It says sit straight up and fasten seat belts. Are we doing it right? Fine."

"Would he like some breakfast?" a stew leans over, "or maybe even a hot dog?"

"I want to go *down*," the child whines, and squirms.

"Sit back and shut up!"

The engines went off. "We stopped," the child says, without a quaver.

"That always happens when we're through climbing," the stew says. "Don't you watch television?"

"I always thought that too when I first flew," the mother said.

"I can't see any lights anymore," the kid says.

"Look out the window," says the stew. "See, we're not stopped."

"Do what the nice lady says, and wave to Daddy and Aunt

WHITE JAZZ

Ella and Chipper." She feels the child's feet relax for an instant but then kick forward with redoubled force. It reminds her of Sandy's competent but programmatic thrusting.

"There's a hole in the wing!" the child yells.

"Those are just flaps, honey," the stew says. "We're leveling off now."

"He got *that* from television," Mother says.

"Hello, Aunt Ella!"

"Don't yell, child. Aunt Ella can't hear you. She's deaf."

"Daddy?"

"You promised your daddy you'd be good. Now read the instructions again. Out loud this time. Come *on,* how about a hot dog, honey?"

The stews are passing up and down the aisle, absorbing the leers and fears, relating the captain's anticipation of turbulence. "Please stay seated," they say. It is getting darker outside. They are going faster than the sun. It isn't fast enough. Outside, on the wing, where the labial ailerons have been retracted, it is written thrice: NO STEP. NO STEP. NO STEP.

"We're going down now, Mama?"

"Yes, dear, we're going down."

"Where to?"

"When we get home, we'll go to the filling station and get some steaks."

"I don't want to go down."

"You can't fly all day. You can't fly any more than to home."

"But I don't wanna go down."

MONDAY

"You didn't want to go *up* before. Maybe you'll grow up to be an astronaut."

"Are we down now, Mama?"

"Not yet." The stew passes a hot dog to the kid.

"Oh, now you've got mustard all over. Wipe it off."

"No."

"Shut up or I'll leave you here. You want to be left *here?*"

"No."

"You want to take the bus home all by yourself?"

"Will Daddy be there?"

"We just said good-bye to Daddy. Be a big boy. Be a man now. Or you'll have to find your own way home."

She lay back. There wasn't much she would have added to that. What man had ever forgotten it? It wasn't the sort of thing one could be intelligent about. She conjures up Sandy above her; with each thrust he closes his light blue eyes. Well, there's something nice about flying, really; about the futility of giving contrary directions at such a height, where fear and toughness are all of a dumb piece. Not at all like coming back from a party with old double-vision Fred, grinding your teeth in the swerving car, wearing out an imaginary brake pedal with a toeless pump from the death seat. The trees that line the road in Fred's wandering lights are the same color as our fuselage...

The child was stamping now. And the man beside her had evidently succeeded in singing himself to sleep, for he was slouched heavily upon her shoulder, an enormous two-tone brogue like a fallen plinth against her calf.

She was just about to request a change in seating when the cockpit reopened and the Captain emerged. He was exceptionally handsome in a stereotypical way, tanned with silvered temples and golden eyes. The Captain touched the bill of his cap over the half-supine lady, but did not look down.

"We have an announcement. There will be increasing turbulence the rest of the way. Please keep your belts on. Also, we're stacked up in an indefinite holding pattern. But if you look out the window," he concluded proudly, "you can see the lights of Akron."

Then as the plane suddenly broke its plane, the Captain smiled self-consciously and braced himself against her seatback. His manicured nails were an inch from her mouth. The child's feet were relentless at her hams. The gentleman to her left had begun to snore. The Captain's hand was ringless, whorled like Sandy's with golden hair and large veins. Large light-blue veins. Also, a raised scar, like Akron from the air, another ganglion of strangulated energy. Like what lay in her lap. Like what kicked her in the back. Like what drove the plane. Like what lit the clouds. Though not enough alike.

The Captain thought the lady was about to scream or vomit. But it was only her suppressed laughter again. Pretty lips drawn up from pretty teeth, offense she was taught not to commit, defense against the tears she would not permit.

'Too many,' she was thinking, 'just too many damn people to love.'

Tuesday

The nerve fibers do not respond to any particular level, but only to changes in the level; the frequency is not directly equal to the intensity of the stimuli, but their monotone function...

OUR MIRROR is flecked with the suds of Sandy's violent toothbrush, gums, like all his tissues, hypostatic from overstimulation. A cloudburst has lengthened the great lawn surrounding the complex of the simple life, the good dirigible, *La V-Bohéme.* The pips of the cherry trees have appeared in one long empyrean smooch. Even the pear, bulldozed, pushed a thousand yards and left on its side in the trash pit, has miraculously rerooted horizontally and is fairly loaded with mauve ovoids. The seasons' functions have been intermingled and accelerated. The fruit blooms twice and the leaves never fall in endless second growth.

But none of this is currently available to the inhabitants. Rather the "outdoors" is, atmospherically, an exact replica of Sandy's steamy bathroom. A great northern front, solid, viscous, and colorless as washed feces has moved in, sucking the dew into a knee-high fog, dregs in which it is not possible to breathe. Sandy determines that it is even unsafe to drive, and checks out his new secret channel on the CB.

The static has become less dramatic, less fulsome, has lost its internal harmonies and reverberations. And there is, well, a kind of voice — unattributable, laconic, indifferent. At first Sandy thinks it's another channel drifting in, but while the tone is casual, it's clear the "person," like the outdoors, is talking to no one but himself. Whoever has been caught unawares, tinkering with his own set, feeling out its spectrum, talking to himself as Adam must have done as he contemplated his dominion, before it became necessary to chat and trade off conversation for sexual favors. The voice makes no literal sense, an androgynous voice unaware of audience, and Sandy must resist the temptation to make contact, to interrupt, to *talk*. This out of a respect for respect, a redundant manners. He regards the equable self-absorbed squabble of human speech at singing play before it became attentive to another. The beginning was not the word. In the beginning was eavesdropping.

He also occupies himself with changing the Color Pak on his kitchenette. Each appliance has four mylar sheets to accent the seasons. Who says there's no free choice? He can have *Winter Wheat,* which he exchanges now for *Spring Spice;* for the summer, *Wilderness Mist* is yet to come, as is *Golden Harvest.* Fall is his favorite time of year, but there's no getting around the fact, strange as it may be, that *Golden Harvest* is the color of puke.

The phone rings and a recorded message reminds him politely that if he will care to look out the window that the haze is in fact lifting, that if he would listen to the appropriate media he

TUESDAY

would learn that the Travelers' Advisory had been waived, and that there is indeed still work to be done even if he is two hours late.

Summoned so peremptorily, Sandy's clock has started over, he ponders how to categorize the human resources of Corrinne L. Huff. "I lacked the three P's," she had said, "Privacy, Passion, and Politics. I have the first, finally; and I'm ready for the second. The third one is a bitch." He can still smell of her, he misses her, he wished he had a response for her, better yet a command; above all, he wished that she did not so devoutly desire categorization — that is what, in his guarded way, which she mistook for the reticence, he was trying to tell her. He scanned the file, from *Asshole* to *Undefeated,* but with so little data to feed, her exponency was quickly determined. The screen flashed *Perdurable* ...ah, put her down under *Perdurable* — not a bad job, that.

Sandy had come to his interest in processing by a passive route. While it was certainly true that his vocational guidance counselors had pressed the field upon him, his motivation was, as they say, negative. For while he had found his schoolmates insufferable overachievers, his mentors were the only men he had ever known who had genuine humility about those processes that both served them materially and interested them conceptually. They affected a strange and imperturbable faith that what excited their curiosity should, by fiat, pay their way in the world — and well. This was an admirable notion. Most of them, like his terrific boss, Haas, were prodigies. Haas himself had doctorates in astrophysics and macroeconomics at the age when all Sandy could think of was snatch and smelled his fingers in the bus to the out-of-town games. Haas at twenty-seven was already assistant director of the Department and kept a harpsichord next to his console in his office. He was all fingertips and mouth. He will, at 30, he says, have a party to celebrate the end of his theoretical intelligence.

It was as if, in their incredibly accelerated lives, these gifted children seemed to understand the perils of curiosity, which in normal people is not curiosity at all, but only a vague and spurious list of options, all ending with *Golden Harvest*. But what Sandy admired most about Haas was his ability to be cheerfully stubborn in the face of the world's ignorance, when the proper and more human response would certainly have been a baleful cynicism or paranoid arrogance. Ah yes, it is not blackheartedness that most offends people, but purity of mind.

Invariably when Sandy met younger faculty from the community college at *El Cielito Lindo,* they dismissed his profession as "genocidal," with the ignorance only people with nothing left but a constricting sense of irony can maintain. They all looked, dressed, and talked alike; they were congenitally incapable of making a first move. Haas was the only person Sandy knew who did not check out *El Cielito Lindo* at least two nights a week. Indeed, as far as he knew, Haas had never been there.

Sandy himself was on the farthest periphery of the computer field, what is known in the trade as a "lumper," as he was overseer of specific processes upon which minds like Haas were dependent, but he was unable to understand the cause, concept, or consequences of the computations underway. Perhaps this is

TUESDAY

why he found *El Cielito Lindo* so salutory — as a kind of temple of temptation to counter the authoritative mystery of the Real Church. Haas chided him, in fact — Haas of the fictional complexion, heavy black glasses, pustules bursting as often as ideas, and a forehead in which the wrinkles were mostly vertical and perfectly parallel — "You'll never be more than a lumper until you quit getting your kicks from asserting your power over the machines. You'll never understand a thing until you relinquish that. You only want to demonstrate power, not receive pleasure."

But Haas was uncharacteristically imprecise about what that pleasure state was like, even with an IQ in excess of 180. "There are only two enterprises that are *in themselves* interesting," Haas says — "describing the world *as if* it were human and describing human behavior in terms *other* than human. The more complex the description, the more expressive of reality. You won't agree with that, I know. Your virtue, you believe, is in your directness."

Haas, in fact, seemed an embodiment of an axiomatic evolution too complex for anyone, including himself, to understand. He behaved as though he was in touch with those tacit assumptions that ruled and described the universe, those space-time frames within which one could observe physical events working out their destinies. It was as if, having the ability to genuinely grasp the uncertainty of physics, he accepted the fact that his work would be forever incomplete. The enormity of this theoretical understanding made him unnervingly calm when making decisions; for Haas, the next best possible guess was quite enough, and the fact that a question lacked evidence was only *proof* that a judgment had to be made and a procedure developed, no matter how arbitrary. "Proof," he said, "is the strangest sounding word we have." He conceptualized as most people walk. He utterly lacked the capacity for self-hatred. He revered his mind precisely because he knew he could never understand how it worked. He knew that his knowledge was more than he could tell, more than he could put into any language, and this fact, so much the topic of fashionable despair at *El Cielito Lindo,* did not appear to concern him in the least.

"The suspension of disbelief is the most difficult thing in the world," Haas warned. "What you'd better remember is that computers have prevented us from thinking hard about ourselves. They have preserved and stabilized institutions that would otherwise have changed or collapsed. Now that we are committed to them, the machines cannot be factored out of the system; like it or not, they're indispensable. No system has meaning unless change is predictable — and within our lifetime, there will be no experience outside of these systems. We wouldn't want any more enigmas, would we?" Then the famous Haas laugh.

Since Sandy's mind was above average, perhaps, but hardly exemplary, he could claim no intellectual fascination with the machines. In fact, on the whole, he found them less predictable than human beings. Most of the people he knew acted far more regularly, predictably, and routinely than even the simplest of the machines, and for this reason he was never in awe of their speed or accuracy, but only their immunity to tedium. Also, it was Haas's observation that Sandy envied the computers because, once integrated in the system, they required *an irreversible commitment;* they could never be removed — and that, not to put too fine a point on it, was what the Sandman desired for himself — not security so much as total synapse. "What we must be willing to concede," Haas warned, "is that our Great American Experiment is a failure. The machines represent our only holding action, until we can admit we have failed and then change ourselves."

It was also true that the basic working principles of the machines, insofar as he could divine them, seemed to tell Sandy more about his own behavior than any history or psychology. He knew very little about the past, his or anyone else's — he knew only that he was hopelessly homogenized, oversimplified, and that distraction was his everyday lot. He was skeptical of his instincts and his training in equal measure. He was certain he had no Superego whatsoever, and not enough of an Unconscious to write home about. He had been told by relatives that there was never a child who took after his father and mother in exactly equal proportions; apparently inheriting both their genetic patterns in bipolar composite. And indeed the basic principle of *their* life had seemed to be that they must produce a creature of greater intelligence and adaptability than themselves. If not twice as smart, Sandy certainly knew twice as much as Tyler and Travis, and, not surprisingly, was at least twice as complicated. This was not, however, what they had in mind. What was clear was that to make his way, then, he needed twice as much power, twice as large a hierarchical structure in which to operate. But lacking what Haas called the "calculus to extrapolate," he knew so very little about his parents that this redoubling of energy seemed mere redundancy. On a fishing trip once, Tyler told him, "Someday I'll tell you about myself," which had literally scared the pee out of the boy, and even when Tyler had died he was extremely relieved that he had forgotten to tell him.

The question was of course one of memory. Ignorance in itself did not bother him; but he was curious whether he never knew or had forgotten. His memory was apparently just as bad as Tyler's and Travis's, though he was measurably superior in every other respect. Haas says, "We are the only animals capable of passing on the subassembly of memory, which is to say we are the only animals who pass on defective memory. It's disgusting to waste so much time pondering where you came from. Technically it is true that a machine cannot feel love, respect, etcetera. It doesn't bother me. Most people don't either. Certainly not the ones who control things. And when I work with the machines, it's simply like working with average normal people, i.e., those who routinely deny their humanity." Then that boyish laugh again.

If you want to understand Sandy (there is ample reason for indifference) all that is necessary to grasp is that he does not work in order to support his leisure, nor does his play relieve the anxieties of his work. Given a choice, he would change neither his work nor his play, nor their relation — he would not know how. In Haas's file, there is his Letter of Reference; *"His interests are wide ranging; his only guidelines, taste and quality"*; his epitaph. Dr. Onarga insists that the only cure for allergy is to substitute another less-damaging addiction. But all the options in the world are unreal to Sandy; what in Haas is professional disinterest produces paralysis in Sandy, a state which his peers pronounce as healthy since it indicates a lack of hang-ups. Sandy's only guilt, in fact, is that he has never felt suicidal.

It was Haas who introduced Sandy to Transistoradentalism, the basic tenets of which are that the differences between mind and machines are clear enough, that there exist sufficient substantive *gross facts* to function perfectly well in the world; that we ought to be damn well comfortable with it and grateful for the stability and structure of what we know, rather than always whining about the lack of some cosmic validity which is strictly literary.

"Precisely because we know so little about the brain," Haas says, "we invariably compare its activity to models we can understand. This is our primordial mistake, the ultimate false science. People always choose the wrong models, flattering ones usually. But the living truth is that everywhere man only meets man; *that* is what this abortion of a century has laid on us! Historically"—Haas always spits this word—"you had to search awhile and 'find yourself.' Now all you have to do is walk right around the corner, don'cha know? There is a new vocabulary for self-expression every turn of the moon. There's a machine somewhere that resembles each and every one of us, and all machines can imitate one another. Me, for example; I'm most like a mass spectroanalyzer, but we won't go into that. My synapses are perfectly circular, which is why I'm so quick. Most people think of themselves as transmitters or receivers, though in our present situation the differences are gradually eradicated. You are neither, Sandy. You are the rare transducer; the only time you feel alive is when you are transferring energy to another system. Yet you are ignorant of both systems. That is why you treat the machine as you do, as an extension of yourself. But you'll never really get anything out of it till you acknowledge its autonomy; such as it is. I've the distinct impression you're capable of that. Look, isn't this how you do?" Haas snatched an envelope and began to draw on the back of it.

"My guess is this. For some reason, genetically — that sounds irrefutable, doesn't it? — you have a loose electron, which wanders in search of positive energy. Also, you have in your system an impurity — like all systems, but *just enough* of impurity, just the *right* impurity; let's call it a hole, or a wandering vacancy. When stimuli are applied, the loose electron is paired with the hole, but when it moves, it leaves a new hole — where it was, see — and the next electron gradually moves into it. That's why you complain so much about your memory. It's not that you've forgotten, so much; it's that the new electron, with its own distinct memory, masks the knowledge of the hole. It's what we call Horizontal Psychology. The holes move negatively; the electrons move positively in the opposite direction. Which is why you can generate considerable power. But energy masks

TUESDAY

memory. That's the bottom line. Now, isn't that a little more believable than Freud? It takes a unique system to handle that — one that's invulnerable to shock, to overheating you might say, because most people are basically made up of material that resists transference. They have the *wrong* impurity. They lack free electrons; they lack, in most cases, even wandering vacancies, although some have too many. Such people break the cosmic circuit; they are deadweight. Isn't that better than Nietzsche? In all probability, your parents each had a semiconductor gene to produce a rectifier like yourself. If you by chance mated with the right woman — statistically minuscule, incidentally — it's possible you could produce an amplifier, a person who could actually control the flow of his holes and electrons at will, a kind of superconductor. Such a person would not only have an unprecedented amount of power at his disposal but, more important, could modulate it synchronously with other systems. Isn't that better than Marx, heh?"

"Would such a child be better at remembering?" Sandy asks, feeling stupider by the minute.

"Such a child would not be self-conscious because he would be completely effective. He would be a kind of true common denominator, totally willful, but egoless."

"That would be difficult to live with."

Haas shrugged. "Both of us, my friend, are rare variations in the blueprint. Might as well make the most of it."

On the ARTS Channel there seems to be a Hispanic, the kind of man women claim not to trust and always get caught with. He is wearing a large amulet about his neck. *Hora Viendra,* he sings, *mi sola hora di gloria.* [My hour is coming. my only hour of glory comes.] Sandy wishes they wouldn't translate everything. Sandy loves languages he doesn't understand. The libretto always spoils things. He strokes himself absently. The Spanish motif seems to be gaining a certain ascendancy.

At *El Cielito Lindo* later, Sandy is surrounded by Skanks; Skanks mocking the cruising salesmen, referencing them in deep whispers, "old cockers, old farts." His drink grinds across the table, his chair gerumps on the floor. There is a buzzing in his ears, a dream of flu, the allergic reaction has taken over, a premonition of a social virus which settles in the frontal lobes; his brain is perspiring like a packhorse into his sinuses, and there are suddenly pointless petty commercials for childhood, manhood, selfhood, and seafood.

He had made the error, earlier on, of ordering the trout stuffed with crabmeat in the *Billy Budd Room,* where the menu is ambivalent and the salad bar is preferable to the monster trout fattened on chows and tagged like a Jew at the gills; the ubiquitous three-bean salad, cottage cheese, dilled onion rings, capers, chow-chow, macaroni salad, groovy Jell-O — he should have stuck to that.

The *Conquerors of Babylon* are playing their newest hit, *Cush:*

> *He shall bruise her head,*
> *And she shall bruise his heel.*

TUESDAY

Maestro Luncheon is working feverishly on the synthesizer; the chords fly out, a cloud of algorithms, an astronomical number of possible chords commingle in the feral air.

Sandy checks out the bulletin board in the foyer. In the *Positions and Situations* section there is a new card.

Successful white man. well off. well put together. and well rested. inclined not to verbalize feelings. wishes previously uninvolved Oriental female physician to 30. for the usual thing.

Tonight Sandy has on a three-piece ice-cream suit and wide pink woolen tie; tonight he is disguised as Peter Muller of Russian/French parentage, a landscape architect at work beautifying the boggling median strip of the expressway. Within an aplomb just short of exquisite, he is explaining to a group of vacationing Midwestern sorority girls the difficulty of moving 150,000 hybrid forsythia with root balls intact which meet the specifications of the state. "Everything now is paperwork," he concludes to a chorus of wows.

As they break for the ladies' room, one remains; one always remains.

"Hi," she says. "I'm finished."

"Aw, come on, you can't be more than twenty-one."

"No, I'm *Finnish*. There's a statue of my great uncle in Helsinki."

"What's his name, love?"

"I can't ever remember it. A big track star."

"Paavo Nurmi!"
"Boy, are you ever smart! I'm Willi. Who's you?"

Tell her about the quaking aspens in Colorado, the rare copper weeping beech of Languedoc, Pierre Moliére, the brittleness of fastigiates, the malleability of the prehistoric ginkgo, Pytor Möller, and the striated Liquidamber, if you are such a man.

On the way back to *The Left Bank,* Willi appears resigned, nearly relieved, in the seasonless air. She mentions she is involved in a relationship which is going to the shits.

They kick off their shoes and pull the gold spread over their knees like a septuagenarian couple with swollen joints taking the cure in Graz, their eyes like embers, unidentifiable cowed animals at the rear of a cave. Willi enjoys thumping the base of the penile shaft; it falls like an oak to her amusement, but then she resuscitates it with an amazing feat. Willi begins skillfully to revivicate the entire National forest, scrambling through the understory, hugging and howling as the shadows begin to jump. "Hey, take it easy," Sandy says. "I've been in the same place you are myself."

In an aureole of haze they lie — footsteps outside in the garden, footsteps down the hall. They have overreached themselves; they have placed themselves at the very center of things. Sandy lies as always, his left arm flung over his left eye. Willi's shoulders have become unbunched. They decide to exchange fantasies.

TUESDAY

"When I think," Willi says, "that others might be watching me give pleasure, that turns me on."

Sandy mulls. "I'm dreaming... I'm President, I'm sitting at my desk. I free the slaves. Then I take a swim in the big pool alone." Sandy confesses that he is not actually Peter Muller.

"I don't care who you are," Willi says.

And in the shower before she rejoins her friends, Sandy can hear her singing one of the *Conquerors'* old hits.

> *Now that the dumb part's done*
> *We can really have some fun.*
> *I'm just as good as new*
> *I'm just as good as you.*

Sandy wishes he had more to say. He has this theory, for instance, that men and women are different, very different, but he cannot prove it; it gets him in trouble, more often than not. The problem seems to be that all the women want to talk about it and the men don't. This mystery is the only true history.

"There's simply not enough data," Haas says. "Quantify and storify. We need more talk!" Sandy wishes he had more to say. He wishes he were a better listener. Haas has devised a basic questionnaire for couples.

PLANNING A STORY OF YOUR OWN
(TO DO BY YOURSELF)

Choose something about which you can make a story to tell your friends. It may be something that has happened to you or someone you know. It may be something you have done, seen, or heard. The following questions may help you:

1. What surprise have you had?
2. What exciting thing has happened to you?
3. What dumb thing have you done?
4. What funny thing has happened to you?
5. What funny or exciting things have you heard on the radio or seen at the movies or on TV?

But Sandy has not yet the guts to hand it out. Each time he simulates the subroutine in the computer, he gets only the most cursory advances.

The assumptions are consistent. Shall I go on?

"I don't get it, Haas! I mean what *is* there to say?"

"Quantify, then storify. You'll never know until you start asking the right questions."

"Can you analyze a steady state, Haas? Everything else around us is growing like crazy, but about *us* we know less than ever."

And then, like a steam cloud from Maestro Luncheon's synthesizer, a typical Haas rejoinder, the penultimate Haasism: "The only people who survive are those whose assets are subject to speculative bidding. What we must be willing to entertain is that we all live at a mean temperature, that each one of us experiences about the same amount of pain, that the voltage of pain is equivalent."

TUESDAY

Sandy lies in the bed gazing upward at his parents at the lake. A wind has come up, a flotilla of sailboats are luffing on a squall line. Upside down his parents seem to have more definition. He goes to the closet to get his pajamas, or rather Tyler's pajamas. He never wore pajamas until Tyler died. He never wears them now except when he is alone and there is no chance of interruption, of his being caught out. The long nightshirt, monogrammed T&T on the pocket, washed a thousand times — there is no crotch in this nightshirt; it falls from the collarbone straight to the floor, it covers his parts with a long fold which begins at the sternum and ends at the ankles.

In the closet, below the pajamas, is Tyler's fishing tackle. Sandy opens Tyler's tackle box, the trays unfold layer by layer; Tyler's crude computer, a stacked memory drum, equidistant rectangles of subjective options; it is a box of memories, a box of philosophy, the sun on his neck, great Canadian steel-colored lakes, rocks exactly the same color and density as the water, dammed southern mountain lakes, their level dictated by electricity demand, rims desiccated with scum and mudflats when the gates are opened to supply our appliances; bobbers, sinkers, serrated knives for fileting, net, scale, mauve plastic worms, pink salmon eggs for the weed beds and stickups, spinners for the sloping clay points, the small handgun to land the meanest muskie of a lifetime. "At dark," Tyler says, "the stripers move into the shallows and the smallmouth leave"; how can a fish believe in this food? Believe that *these* are brothers and sisters, these lures with glaucomic eyeballs and hinged midsections? Is it the same necessary suspension of belief that bubbles the silty waters of *El Cielito Lindo* Reservoir — a thousand lures and not a single fish? The lures are roiling in the air, out of their element, their resistance is not conclusive. Their motion, their dance, does not whet the appetite; and perhaps that is the secret — that their attraction lies in the fact that they are wholly and equally unconvincing. They leap out of their respective plastic rectangles to wiggle and scrooge, adopt their new names — *Hell Riser, Baby Torpedo, Darter,* and our good friends, *Creek Chub Plunker* and *Deep Dive Runt.*

Sandy takes the lures and throws them one by one, throws them desultorily against the plashing streamlet. They do not stick in that stylish water and slide routinely by natural laws to the field of orange shag. Sandy has never been fishing without Tyler. He has had no reason to fish without Tyler. Fishing actually seemed a little silly to Sandy, even with Tyler. What is he going to do with all this *equipment* — seven rods for the seven oceans, for God's sake, two tackle boxes? Fish must really be bored to go for that stuff.

Haas gets peeved when Sandy puts Tyler's and Travis's wasted assets through the computer: their obituaries, the baby books, the trunks of wartime letters, the bills, the years of income tax, every canceled check including two audits, and the enormous file of letters of respectful and *pro forma* consolation from people Sandy did not know.

Haas objects. "You can neither locate nor disembody memory," he says, "you can only forget it. On this matter, we are as ignorant as the Greeks."

TUESDAY

A lot Haas knows in the end; all Sandy is trying to do is process the information faster, information that would otherwise take him a lifetime to reflect upon; for to speed up, accelerate remembrance exponentially, is finally, to escape it — there's a Haasism for you, Haas. But if these emotions are *incalculable,* Haas — like you say, Haas — if confused emotions are slave emotions, then why not submit them to a slave function, eh, Haas? I don't want them anymore. Put them on *tape,* I say. It is for others to retrieve them! "It is quite conceivable," Haas ends it, "that these complexities play no useful role at all. But not to worry; there is always a period of grace...of summation ...whether you want it or not."

The left arm is thrown over the left eye again, but this time the eye moistens the arm, not the other way around; what froth remains is his alone. Was it because he had ignored their lives that he was now destined to dwell upon their deaths? And then, finally, Sandy dreams — knowing, as always, that it is a dream, a dream of a dream, a chimera of Tyler's and Travis's "life," of how he imagines Tyler dying — because surely he did not die, just falling over like that on the ninth hole, while his lawyer friends muttered that it was against the law to give in contemplation of death?

Tyler hoisted the red chair on his stomach as Travis held the porch door, thighs and trapezius taut as guy wires, his feet hidden from him as he walked. The door rocketed shut as he cleared it. Tyler screamed at Travis, but the chair's bolster muffled it.

Tyler looked up and down the street. The Dibbles were

throwing away clothes the dog had chewed, and a pole lamp. The Morrisons were throwing out a mildewed wicker ottoman, picture books with warped bindings, and a stone. Tyler surmised the stone was not being thrown away but only holding down something that was. The Williamses were throwing away hangers, a ream of frayed twine, a great quantity of newspapers, and a wagon wheel. The Forresters were throwing away an orange crate, a portable bar that had apparently burned up, and several lengths of anodized aluminum drainpipe. The Thompsons were throwing away carpeting undercarpeting, carpet cleaner and carpet tacks, wallpaper, plasterboard, outer light fixtures, and a rusty green tricycle. There were other less attributable piles all the way to the corner.

Tyler got a playful nudge from behind. "You forgot the cushion," Travis said, dropping it at his feet. "If we're going to get rid of the chair, let's not leave the cushion around."

Tyler snatched up the cushion, made like to hit her back, then flung it into the chair.

"You really think they're going to pick up all this junk for nothing?" he said.

"Anything two men can carry," Travis cried over her shoulder. "That's what they said."

Anything unpulpable you had to get rid of yourself.

Propped like an omen out against the garbage cans, still the garbage people wouldn't touch that old headboard. It had taken Tyler a week to get rid of it all. It was rock maple. He had to chop it into pieces to fit it into the incinerator. Each piece had to be soaked in gasoline and then, by law, he had to watch each

TUESDAY

piece burn. Even if there was no law he had to watch it burn anyway, to prevent the Dibbles' magnolia from getting singed. Dibble's tree hung over his incinerator and the smoke went up through it like God's own muffler. He had given a good deal of thought to the legal complications of this, even to the extent of having one of the boys at the firm do some research for him. He knew that if the magnolia were a fruit tree and some fruit dropped over on his property, he was entitled to pick it up, though he was not allowed to pick it *from* the tree even if it occupied his air space. But then, he figured, if the smoke did not go *across* Dibble's property line but straight *up*, where the tree was alleged to bloom, then could not his infrequent smoke rising be interpreted in the same light as Dibble's hypothetical falling fruit?

Travis often watched Tyler thinking out there, silhouetted against the night fire of the incinerator, her husband's own winking cigarette the focus of the conflagration. She had decided to get rid of the chair on just such a night, after sinking into it to watch the washer. The dancing clothes in the round window had reminded her of spring cleanup. When Tyler got back from the club, she had told him to carry out the chair. After he had carried it out, though, and she had come upon the pillow he had forgotten, she had second thoughts. It was an English club chair they had bought just after their honeymoon. Red leather, presynthetic, it had aged to a deep splotched orchid hue. She never used it, even when Tyler was at work, because she liked to put her feet under her when she sat, and when her feet started to sweat, the leather would get exotically slippery. Monthly saddle-soap baths could not keep Tyler's body from wearing it out, discoloring it with night sweat. Finally Tyler seemed to wear out the very notion, the *being,* of the chair. When he got up, the indentation of his body didn't rebound for days. And when they came back from two weeks in the Bahamas and his prevacation dents still had not been absorbed, Travis told him to take the chair to the basement. She sat in it down there when her back got tired from watching the washer.

Making highballs later, Tyler asked Travis, "How do you suppose they pulp a chair?"

"I expect they will rummage it, dear, or give it to one of those places where cripples make it over."

"Well, they'll have to get a different truck. They sure as hell can't pick it up in the pulper."

"They *have* the trucks, Tyler," Travis snapped. "Don't you worry one minute about that. They've got the trucks."

Tyler carried the highballs into the den. Travis came in and for some reason put her head in his lap. "Remember when you tried to cut up the mattress?" she giggled, and snitched from his drink.

Tyler crossed his legs expertly beneath his wife and nodded. They had tried, Lord knows, to give away the old mattress with the headboard when Travis decided to get twin beds, but there was a law against used mattresses, so they had left it behind the garage, where it had become rain soaked and consequently unliftable.

"So wet's already pulp and that'll jam the pulper sure, to

TUESDAY

put what's already pulp in it," the garbage people said.

So Tyler let the mattress dry for a week or so in the sun and then tried to chop it into incinerator-sized pieces. But the axe sprang back, and his upswing became more vigorous than his downswing. Then Travis suggested the shears, and with one of them snipping and the other chasing down enormous fluffs of escaped stuffing, they worked until most of it was finally in the "incin," as Travis called it.

"Anything else you want out?" Tyler asked.

Travis shook her head. Breezes cooled the whole house.

Usually when Travis washed her hair it made her look younger, but late that night it didn't. She stamped into the den looking merely wet and worn out.

"Tyler, there's somebody fooling around in the front."

Tyler looked at her from the very tops of his eyes.

"I heard them from the bathroom, I tell you. They're going to take the chair."

"Who'd want the chair, hon? We couldn't give it away."

"Look, that's a fine chair, and there's a lot of people who would like to get their hands on it you can bet, and there's somebody out in the yard right now thinking about it."

"What the hell. Who cares who takes it as long as it's gone."

"Tyler, if you think for one minute that I'm going to stand for someone to walk right in here and take what's ours..."

"Matter of fact, Trav, it just occurred to me that the parkway is public property. We're obliged to keep it clean, of course, but if perchance a pedestrian should find a hundred-dollar bill on the parkway outside our house, there isn't a court in the world..."

"Tyler, if you don't get those strangers out of the goddamn yard, I'm going to call the cops."

Tyler looked after Travis as she disappeared up the staircase, then went into the foyer and parted a starched curtain. There was a white station wagon parked before the house and there was indeed movement about it. He could hear Travis above him taking a last rinse, though still apparently listening for his pending action through the rush of water. He drew in his breath and went out to the kitchen.

Laying various utensils before him on the cutting board, he determined that the most efficient weapons couldn't be hidden, while those he could secrete on his person did not seem sufficiently threatening when and if withdrawn. He finally decided upon an anniversary corkscrew, a reindeer and chrome auger which he could fit within his jacket pocket without mutilating himself. Then he slipped quietly out the front door.

The station wagon was cruising slowly up the street now. As its windows were dark in the moonlight, he presumed it was full of people. The chair was lashed securely to the roof of the car. It stopped again before the Dibbles' pile.

Tyler found himself running toward them, a cry stuck in his throat, right hand jammed in his jacket pocket. As he neared, the car accelerated, ran the stop sign, and careened out of sight.

Tyler returned to the house to find Travis in the doorway, hair in curlers, arms afold, kimono-clad.

TUESDAY

"For a lawyer," she said, "you certainly don't have much respect for the law."

She confronted him on the sidewalk. Her shivering in the night air was catching.

"I never thought I'd see the day when I wouldn't feel safe in my own front yard."

Tyler retreated from her, staggering slightly, and as he did so, Travis emitted a triumphant cry. "The pillow! Son of a bitch, Ty, they forgot the pillow."

Tyler slumped into himself and looked like he was listening.

"They wouldn't take a fine piece like that and leave the pillow, I'll tell you. They'll be back, all right." She was ecstatic.

"But, Trav, they saw me coming..." Tyler balled up his fist in his pocket.

"Don't tell me, Tyler. I know their kind. They'll be back, and when they do, we'll be ready for them."

Tyler's head cleared, his heart ceased roaring.

"Well, I won't have a thing to do with it. I divest myself of all..."

She stalked away from him, and wrapping her kimono about herself, squatted deliberately down among the evergreens which bordered their lot.

"Can you see me, Tyler? Tell me now."

"Of *course* I can see you."

"No. From the front," she shrieked, "if you were in a car, say."

Tyler walked to the grassy parkway and did an about-face.

"Well, no. Not very well."

"Okay. Pillow there?"

"Pillow there, Trav," he said quietly.

"Okay, now, *divest* yourself!"

Tyler went back into the house and down to the basement. There he began methodically to carry large, carefully tied bundles of newspapers and rags out to the incinerator. He made several trips, and when the pit was filled, he slung his jacket over his shoulder and tossed a kitchen match into the rubbish. A curtain of flame rose up, enveloped Dibble's magnolia in a corona of ornamental fire. Then it subsided. Ribbons of newsprint slithered orange and diaphanous through the trees and out toward the stars. Enameled sheets of advertising carbonized before his eyes, floated like chiffon in the smoke, powdered against the underside of the branches. The sweet smoke in his nose elated him like scotch and soda. His good heart was knocking him about.

Tyler stood in the shadows at the rear of the pit, eyeing the clump of evergreens that concealed his wife. Looking up the side yard, the pillow appeared as some undersea sponge trap in the moonlight. He heard a car turn the corner, but remained by the fire as the white station wagon reappeared at the front of the house and doused its headlights.

Then, as if on a prearranged signal, Travis rose out of the bushes. Her kimono billowed from her arms, her curlers were undone. Strands of damp hair uncoiled across her face. Tyler strained forward but could hear nothing over the roar of the fire. Travis's arms were going up and down like semaphores. The

TUESDAY

car's windows were lowered menacingly and then raised halfway. Tyler left the fire to face them.

One foot on the pillow and with a knee against its white flank, Travis berated the phlegmatic auto. Tyler walked around to the driver's side to have a look.

"Hello, there," he said affably, and extended his hand through the half-open window. Nothing grasped it. All he saw was

Teeth & Eyes

"What's your name, hey?" he continued, feeling about in the gloomy interior.

Teeth & Eyes

"Trav," Tyler raised his voice and withdrew his hand, "if you will kindly stop yelling, perhaps our visitors can explain what they want."

Travis howled at her husband's famed politeness as Tyler again peered through the window. Then a high soft voice spoke from within the car.

"You motha you."

Tyler dropped his hand into his pocket. He would twist the anniversary corkscrew right between the malevolent eyes and the blood would envelop his fist like a carnivorous flower.

Tyler did not know how many he had to contend with. He stepped away from the car to check the back seat. But the rear window was closed and he could see only his own face eclipsing the moon in the glass. Retreating ever farther, he wondered how they had gotten the chair up on the car without scratching it. It faced backward, lashed tight with clothesline, girdled in complicated professional knots. He thought of Egyptian slaves, inclined planes, and golden rope.

The moon went behind a cloud, taking his face with it, and the glass cleared. Then he saw that the back seat had been folded flat and on it, surrounded by his neighbors' discarded personal effects, lay a lovely dark girl. She wore blue jeans and a man's undershirt. Her small hard breasts peeped from shoulder holes shaped for pectoral muscles. Her waist was soaked with perspiration. For a moment he believed he recognized the Morrisons' potted geraniums and a portion of the Forresters' rose arbor. But as the moon reappeared so did his face, initially as a ghost crowned with fire and ultimately, as the glass again mirrored, a Technicolor refraction which absorbed the dark girl.

From the other side of the car, Travis's moans were growing fainter. Awed by his own indolent image before him, Tyler decided to get to the root of the matter.

"Well," he said, leaning against the door casually, "how about some identification?" There was some shuffling in the car's interior, and finally a wallet was belligerently thrust from the window.

Despite the many Plexiglas containers, it was empty save for a single business card. The card read:

DUMP — PICKUP — DUMP

Tyler drew in his breath. All his interior organs seemed to be swelling.

TUESDAY

The wallet was snatched back into the car and an unintelligible conversation ensued. Travis, who had by now moved in behind him, snorted.

At last the high soft voice which had first spoken spoke again.

"You gunna call the *po*lice yoo?"

Travis smiled and clasped her hands.

"It's none of my concern," Tyler said. "Actually, you are welcome to the chair, but the law was made for a reason and you're breaking it."

"You better put that chair right back where you found it," Travis yelled behind him. Tyler motioned her to be quiet and then they both stepped back from the station wagon to see what would happen.

The car swayed slightly on its overloaded springs, but there was no conversation. Tyler wondered about the girl, if she were really boss, what they would do with the junk. She'd look just fine, he thought, curled up in the corner of that red chair in big rich old white man's underwear.

"Trav," he whispered, "why don't we just let them have it?"

She looked, to him, sweet for the first time in years, and then all her strength seemed to evaporate.

"It was silly, really, to throw it away."

When he was younger, Tyler reflected, he would have had them all arrested. He knew what his life had been like.

Confident they would not dare to expose themselves in the well-lighted street, Tyler mounted the rear bumper and hauled himself, with considerable difficulty, to the roof of the car. As he stretched past the rear window, he caught a glimpse of the dark princess through the gilded glass. She was lying on her stomach and elbows, breasts bunched beneath her like expiring party balloons, making a plaything of coat hangers and corkscrew. On all fours, Tyler jabbed violently at the ropes with the corkscrew. A strand began to unravel and he rested. He could see the last coals of the incinerator from his vantage point. Dibble's magnolia glowed, bloomed, through the smoke. Travis, calmer now, refolded her arms and smiled benignly up at him. Tyler's jacket was soaked. He worked frantically at another rope.

At first he thought it was simply the princess gone berserk beneath him; the roof of the car had buckled slightly and he could hear her sighing up to him through the concave steel. But when he saw Travis drawing imperceptibly away from him, he knew he was moving.

As she became smaller, her mouth enlarged and her arms dropped helplessly at her sides. The acrid smell of burning rubbish filled his nostrils, and advocate Tyler was flung in a burst of shifting gears back into the chair. Only then did the trees tell him of the speed. The Dibbles', Morrisons', Williamses', Forresters', and Thompsons' flickered peripheral to sight, then recongealed in the familiar distance. He tried to grasp an overhanging branch but it broke off in his hand. Then, very deliberately, as Travis was absorbed into the darkness, Tyler settled back, loosened his belt, stretched his legs, and, grasping the arms of his favorite chair, allowed the terrible wind to course up his pant legs.

Wednesday

As the stimuli become more and more similar,
learning takes more trials...

THE FRONT had lifted as suddenly as it had come. The grass refamiliarized itself to those who walked upon it; everything had seemed to recover its proper density, if not gravity, as the marvelous mass of thick mist was dismantled. The grass is there because of its word, just as the seas are held back by the word. We must admit our lack of knowledge on this point, this sea of sterile herbs; so much in the world that you cannot eat! The close-fitting lawns are a kind of punishment; in the words of *The Conquerors,*

> *a river of grass by the door,*
> *but no nightingale in this sycamore.*

On his way to the Pontiac, Sandy spied a man doubled over in the dappled shade of a honeysuckle hedge. He approached cautiously, then broke into a trot as he recognized him. Art Entelechy was vomiting into the bees and greenness.

"Art, you okay?"

The large stocky man grasped his thick knees; his knuckles were badly skinned. He nodded affirmatively as he retched.

"You sure, Art?"

The nodding became more vigorous, with a grotesque twist of the head which indicated a request for privacy which Sandy honored.

Art Entelechy, quarterback of the Rough Grouse, had only recently moved into *The Left Bank,* the most recent victim of the home-buster syndrome of *El Cielito Lindo.* Prominent athletes such as Art had been attracted to the lounge like everyone else, and ultimately he had taken up with one of Wanda June's peers, a squirrely Skank by the name of Moira. Mrs. Fran Entelechy, upon discovery of this lapse on her famed husband's part, kicked him out of the house, attaching a goodly portion of his $500,000 annual salary on behalf of their three attractive children. Art now lived with Moira in her *Left Bank* efficiency.

Entelechy had taken to Sandy because Sandy never discussed sports and was perhaps the only person who had never once acknowledged Entelechy's professional identity, despite the fact that, secretly, Entelechy was the only athlete who could sustain Sandy's interest. Of all the professionals Sandy had encountered, Entelechy was the only one who utterly lacked an identifiable and calculated style. While his efforts were wholly predictable because he was so consistent, the way he achieved them varied not only from game to game but from quarter to quarter. Every time you tuned him in, he was different — at one moment a hunchbacked scrambler, at another, a poised dropback pin-pointer, with cunning regressions to the split-T roll-out lumper of his college days — unrecognizable if it wasn't for his number, though his seasonal statistics never varied by more than a factor of 5 percent. It was as if Entelechy were driven, not by a desire to surpass himself or even win, but by infinitely varied disguise, to put himself at one remove from the image his celebrity conferred on him.

Sandy's low opinion of Moira was confirmed by Entelechy's silent suffering, without a trace of self-pity, manifesting itself in the symptoms we have just witnessed and having more to do with his overbearing mistress and receding family than the coming play-off game on Saturday, the twelfth time in thirteen seasons that the Grouse had been involved in post-season play. Sandy did not understand Moira's physical attraction either, having once experienced her desperate, despondent, balled-fisted heaving, and even more enervating, her 'open and upfront' manner: i.e., "A man talks to you more if you play with his cock." She believed her sullenness to be a breakthrough in our most recent genderocide. It was difficult for Sandy to imagine how anybody could leave a family, a four-car family yet, for a mortification such as Moira. He recalled Haas's warning, tongue in cheek though it was: "Unless what you do to a woman is not formulated with the greatest precision and care, you will be punished. Usually not immediately, however. The historical lack of societal-role strength makes it necessary for them to accumulate hatred in a measure that cannot be quantified, much less imagined, in the male stoical mode."

Art's explanation of marriage was less scientific if more convincing. "It's like a wrestling match I had in high school once. With a blind boy. At first you don't fight too hard because you don't want to take advantage. But you end up fighting harder than ever because you don't want a handicapped person to beat you at anything."

"What I've done," Art said as they watched a late-nite movie together, "is traded in a '58 Chevy for a '59 DeSoto."

Sandy's was the only place where Entelechy could get away from both his dependents and his reporters. When Art came to visit, Sandy would lay out the lightest of scotch single-malts and burliest of beers, and they would talk ingeniously around the subjects of sport and sex, drinking and laughing to excess, occasionally grasping each other's knees and forearms. "Things don't change," Entelechy once sighed, "they just get more and more the way they are."

As an athlete, Entelechy's notable achievement was his consistency, and "Mr. Constancy" was the nickname the Grouse front office had laid on him. If he had never had a truly great game, he had never had anything approaching a bad one. This perhaps made him less memorable than he deserved.

Sandy left his vomitous friend reluctantly. As the Pontiac pulled out, Entelechy had sat down on the grass and crossed his cartilaginous legs. His polo shirt was soiled with spittle.

It was from Art Entelechy, quarterback and philanderer, that Sandy had learned the perils of replication. He had lost his only possible hero through a series of technological refinements which he never would fully comprehend. It had begun with instant replay, a process that had initially caused him to lose concentration on the game itself, and indeed he believed it had affected his perception of things in general. He tended to be

WEDNESDAY

amazed when things were not repeated, and he knew that regarding the world from all possible angles had made him unwary, that such perspective had, in fact, become a substitute for any considered judgment. He resented particularly his dependence upon "The Highlights" — an anthology of the games of the week. But as Art was only one of sixteen other quarterbacks, as well as the most consistent (which is to say, the least dramatic) his progress was not often highlighted. An ultimate humiliation occurred one evening when Sandy turned on the tube and saw Entelechy dropping back in slow motion, only to be felled by a blitzing back's subcutaneous swipe across the face guard, our hero's legs spasming up in a slow spiral until he was standing on his head, the ball squirting loose and bouncing out of camera range, and there, at the very top of this undignified arc he is stalled, frozen by the megalomaniacal director, who then runs the film *backward* — the tackle runs backward, the ball bounces back into the picture, into Entelechy's trembling hands, the background music changes from semiclass to high-funk, and then the Great Collage is assembled — snippets from History's Great Games, *25 years ago today*, a funny short man running the length of the foreshortened field like a catarapid in a cartoon; and final indignity of all, Entelechy's head appears, superimposed upon the body of a Grouse — the bird has the team turtleneck sweater on, but is naked from the sweater down, with no genitalia but hyperextended bandy legs with dewlaps. "I'll tell you about myself sometime," is what Art always said.

If Art and Sandy had been brought together by sex's fallout, Sandy and Haas also obliquely comforted one another. Haas was concerned about his colleague's "predilection for predation," that the middle class would destroy itself to the extent that its erotic behavior came to resemble that of the rich and the poor. For Sandy, to test Haas was to cheerfulize his carnality; at the end of each working day, he would invariably leave him a memo of supportive commands....

WHAT YOU DO WITH A GIRL, HAAS

1. Ruggedize existing systems.
2. Circumvent random memory with single instruction stream.
3. Exercise patience if gate delay. Proceed.
4. Reach nonzero state gradually.
5. Take into account parasitic impedance of passive elements, power dissipation, and intrinsic delay.
6. Avoid bipolar relationships which are faster but require enormous energy reserves.
7. Nonvolatilize memory. Proceed.
8. Negatize resistivity. Proceed.
9. Technify response times.
10. Match access time with logic circuit speeds.
11. Instigate associative array process.
12. Clear all registers!
13. Tie in sense amplifiers with output registers.
14. Reevaluate potential integrals through iterative process.
15. Interrogate need function.
16. Correlate trends. Proceed.
17. Extrapolate viability.
18. (Viability=availability, reliability, maintainability, flexibility.)
19. Observe Yes, And/Or No gates. Proceed.
20. When costs and size are determined, trade-offs are available.
21. Once convergent trends are established, initiate subroutine.
22. Interleave the interface!
23. Think of yourself as sapphire on silicone.
24. Simplify interface.
25. Initiate consensual trade-offs.

26. Buffer memory. Proceed.
27. Try asynchronous ripple carry.
28. Recall. (The larger the memory, the greater the parasitic impedance and reduction of response time.)
29. Initiate fault detection.
30. Read real time. Proceed.
31. Sponsor backup system.
32. Increase transparency to alleviate software problems.
33. Fault detection. Proceed.
34. Exercise fault toleration.
35. Bubble.
36. Compile command junction in cylindrical domain.
37. Roll back.

"Haas, why would anyone want to simulate something like the *mind?* Jeez-*us!*"

"Remember, Sandy," Haas said very patiently, "that God was sorry he made man, but the fact he was sorry, didn't make him change his mind."

Sandy glummed. Nothing, not even the most up-to-date humor would make Haas smile.

"You must stop thinking of women as phenomena that pass into your field of vision and then get in the way of your will. I say that, not out of some spurious sense of fairness, but only as a warning to you... for all of your activity, I doubt you have ever fucked anyone with the same character defects as yourself. This is the true test..."

"Haas, these aren't problems between men and women. This is no Don Juan stuff, believe me. These are... family problems."

Haas was delighted at this.

"Hey, that's it. Don't sell yourself short! You are all birthing, you fools, birthing! Despite the fact you loathe and fear children. All those ingenious Japanese catcher's mitts to catch the curdled milk — no, the dampened palm will not save you, Sandman. There will be...growths...nonwithstanding!"

"I don't follow you..."

"What we must be willing to entertain is that we are adapting biochemically to a new condition. Only our Technology will allow us to survive this long evolution. The ideas we hold about ourselves as a species are very, very recent. I believe we have in our cytoplasm the potentiality of producing a new appendage — a third sensor, a satellite intelligence, a further expansion of the frontal lobe, the eye of which is now only turned upon ourselves in its embryo stage, but will eventually lose its puppy interest in us and turn its apprehension upon the world, gaining its own identity. Dualism will become unthinkable, the legal and clinical definition of the clearly retarded...God made you people scatterbrained and wide-eyed so that you could grow something *new* there. The mammal adapts by projecting itself..."

Understandably, Sandy could never respond to Haas directly, and he hated himself for not being able to counter with those one-liners that invariably occurred to him several days after his last conversation. But as he swam his lengths that afternoon, pondering Haas's meditations on ladies and New Growths, his thoughts wandered to Wanda June, recalling one of their recent luncheon meetings. On his fortieth lap, he had formulated a response to Haas along these lines:

WEDNESDAY

"The point you refuse to understand, Haas, and which conditions do not permit explaining, is that in fact men like myself are fascinated finally and only by machines; not tools, but women's machinery. Mystery sure. Romance sure. Release sure. But the *whole idea of the thing,* that's what's missed, when you open up the hood and look down on that engine! It's just ...*there,* by God! Does this make me a bad man, Haas? And their problems, their *bouts.* Christ, how do they stand it!"

How many times had he lain with Wanda June on her days off, massaging her swollen feet, listening stoically to the things she could never tell her lovers or doctors.... It seemed a natural extension of his job to mediate between the scientific speculation and bemused terror which focused so ineffectually upon that small lovely place of the short ugly word. The chronic low-grade infections, as palpable and incurable as the flu, flu of the wazoo is what she called it, with such good cheer and forbearance. Although it was clear that she was capable of granting exquisite pleasures, it seemed to Sandy that her very trust in him would require their forbearance, a rectitude which astounded him in its simplicity.

She had confessed at that last luncheon that she had a new complication, and he ran his finger over and about that curious webbing, so much like the clouds, where she feared for cysts, he traced the tiny scar over the impacted Bartholin gland, a bit of bruised fruit.

Can you feel it?
Yes. But you told me to look for it.
Will it make a difference?

I doubt it. Not if you're excited.

Am I ugly there?

God no.

But in comparison…?

Wanda June, I know this sounds idiotic…but they're *all* beautiful.

That can't be. It must be, just a notion of yours…

I wasn't being romantic…

What about old ones?

Well, I've never seen an old one.

Wanda June smiled.

You know, with you, Sandman, I can almost accept the fact that things will never work out for me.

Don't say that.

Somebody around here has to be realistic.

In that spirit, there is one thing that strikes me.

Yes?

A general observation, you understand.

Yes?

But I don't know if we should speak of it.

Come on, hey, I can take it.

Well, it's about…the there…

The there?

You know, for God's sake. Don't embarrass me.

Well, yes, go on.

Well, is it not…a bit…misplaced? Not yours alone…I mean generally.

Wanda's eyes widened.

WEDNESDAY

Not that it's unsurmountable, of course, but...
But what?
Well, couldn't they have just dropped it down a bit, I mean, even half an inch...?
I see what you mean. Sort of.
I mean I don't get it. Was it to separate the men from the boys, the concerned from the casual?... If that's so, why do they make fun of us when we act like men?
Well, Wanda said brightening, it's too late to worry about it now. Right? I mean it's like trying to be less self-conscious or something.
You're admirable.
I'll tell you something that's more interesting, if you want to know.
Sure.
Well, it's hard to put in words, but it's like I'm growing something new.
Oh Wanda. Christ, not again. Jesus! What luck, what a life...
Not *there*, dummy. That's what's so weird about it.

And then she went on to relate in considerable detail and with unaccustomed force, yet another SIDE EFFECT, as usually related to menstrual flow which had abated *pax in bello,* but had also produced what she had first thought were simply spots before her eyes, a commoner's dizziness, but she had gradually come to believe that these motes were more alive somehow than either herself or the landscape they occupied. She described it, unfortunately perhaps, as something like a tongue which began where the neck joins the back, in Wanda June's case, one of the most remote and unspoiled areas left on the East Coast, and from there it seemed to follow the curvature of the skull, something like a plume, until what were spots congealed, took shape, and dangled before the eyes, particularly in times of confused adrenal activity. So she was growing one too, and for once in the same place as his.

This confirmation of the Haas phenomena could only heighten Sandy's awe. Dripping on the edge of the pool, he saw Wanda June through the glass partitions of the dining room, the hot roll tray against her belly, appearing in panel after panel, making time.

He felt that he was in the presence of the future of the race.

In return for the Supportive Commands, Haas has left him a new video game, for home, office, and the car; the subroutine simple but challenging.

HOW TO TRAVEL IN FUN

Count all animals along the highway. All animals count one point. If there is a school or a church on the player's side of the road, double their score. If a cemetery is passed on your side of the road, you must start all over again. One player starts a word with a letter. Each of the other players adds a letter. The object of the game is to avoid completing the word. The person who is

WEDNESDAY

forced to complete a word becomes a third of a ghost. Some players may not actually have a word in mind. They can be challenged. If a challenged person does not have a word in mind, he also becomes a third of a ghost. Those who become full ghosts cannot remain in the game. Only one person who is not a full ghost can win.

There is a warning on the box:

> Se sustituirán las piezas que presenten defectos de material o de acabado así como aquellas piezas están deterioradas forzosamente por causa de dichos defectos. Las piezas sustituidas pasarán a ser propiedad del vendedor y habrán de ser entregadas a la misma. Made in Puerto Rico.

Sandy weeping. The trouble with proceeding is that it tends to be prolonged. Let us have, Haas, a period of summation. Wednesday always makes Sandy weak. Jumpy. Touchy. He has come home too early on weak Wednesday. Miswired with satiation, he glances at the ceiling, at the blue cubicle of air beyond the window, at the photos, no not the photos, he is suddenly screaming into the secret channel, foul curses, denunciations, guttural cries of astonishment and bewilderment, those first words in the garden when it was discovered that the Tree of Life is deciduous... The reply is equable, even. He has made contact:

Shit, fuck, cock, balls! What do you think of me *now*?

Now watch your lingo there. good buddy. We don't want to lose this channel do we? Isn't it nice to have a private place to talk?

"..."

Got nothing to say for yourself, huh? Just a little cussin' will do ya, huh?

"..."

Let's try and be businesslike about this. First I'll give you some safety information. Down at milepost 181 there's a guy playing golf with himself on the median strip. So watch your windshield...

I'm not on the road, you idiot.

I know where you're at, Sandman. Don'tcha know who this is? Good buddy?

Maintenance Man! Where the hell are you? I got trouble hearing you. Turn down the music!

It ain't *my* music, mister. All the music means is that you're connected. This station's fucked up with nuts.

When you due back? The toilets are all backing up. And somebody's got a dog...!

When the moonlight's over, honey. I can't make it on what you pay...

WEDNESDAY

On the ARTS Channel, in the dusk, leafless vertiginous poplars scrape in pastoral. There is another Spanish man singing in the shower, covered with enormous glistening soap bubbles, the sub-titles running across the base of the tub.

"Una oscura pradera me convida, sus mentales estabales y ceñidos..." [An obscure meadow lures me, her vast close-fitting lawns...]

Sandy would prefer that events are better connected than they are. 'No more information, please' he thinks; even prays.

It's Fish and Fowl Night at the Wharf Rat. Sandy cares for neither. The Wharf Rat wears Bermuda shorts, an ascot, horn-rimmed glasses, and a beret. He points out the choice on the place mat, a frozen flounder stuffed with Rock Cornish game hen or vice versa. Or crepes. Or the famous sushi pasta. The Wharf Rat is dancing on his hind legs, more of a frug than your conventional cavort. Having left all fours late in his evolution like us, he will have nothing but lower back pain for this effrontery. The Wharf Rat counts one point for Sandy.

Sandy noted the *Positions and Situations* board as he nervously entered *El Cielito Lindo* at ten on the dot.

Very attractive healthy handy elastic divorced young woman desires life companion for courtship. Age or looks not that important. What I lack in experience I make up for with enthusiasm. Am seeking serenity-seeking man, realistic and slender, who will love and respect his special person. No creeps, sissies, or crusaders. Monogamous, nonmacho relationship, must know goals. be past planning. have financial security. Desire nothing but peace. quiet. and hard work. I'm tired of having God do the choosing for me. Help me with a punch line.

The Dreamer

Sandy had never lied to a woman in his life, and it was precisely this fact which made his seductions so effortless. Actually, any promiscuity on his part could only be viewed as part of a larger asceticism. If one was to believe Haas, whatever the girls found in him was generated by some very crude electricity — which, if only channeled, could focus on the most profound questions of existence — but in his case had only acted kinetically to date, like those diffuse globes which illuminate nothing save the moths attracted to them. Maybe it was better to lie and be caught at it than loved like that.

When he saw her, though, alone at a table, he ceased questioning himself: a pink lady with guitar. She was one of those blondes darkening; face done with arm-length scoops, eyebrows that would grow together if not plucked, veins like water beads upon an amber tumbler, ears pierced aristocratically with mismatched pearls. When she reads, she bites her nails and tucks her feet beneath her buttocks. She walks slashingly, legs so formidable that her arms seem perfectly dispensable. She does not know the difference between education and experience, her mouth is farthest open when she is silent, she doesn't know which is her best feature, and when she lies down there is nothing like a pie.

Tonight there will be no formalities, familiarities. Tonight there will be no evaluation. Tonight he is a violist on his way to a Hindemith retrospective in Manila. He has to practice eight hours a day. He hasn't time to fool around. *The Conquerors* are stomping out *Cut and Paste* polka:

> *And on my wafer*
>   *I'll put your chip*
>   *Then I'll take my life…*
>   *Down to old Mexico*

She stood now in Sandy's vestibule in an elderly camel's-hair coat, too short for her long legs, too heavy for the season, the nap dry-cleaned to a patchy blond pelt, like her once fine hair, now brittle from a protracted adolescence of permanent waves.

"You look a little pale," he said.

"I'm nervous," she said.

He helped her off with her coat, conscious of the light damp hair whorled at her nape. She had on a new dress, a crimson stretch-shorty, with panels cut out exposing her hips. Her front hairs were swept into a kind of horizontal bouffant, eye sockets sprinkled with sequins, lips tumescent, fried, and frosty. In one hand she carried a manila portfolio; in the other, Lord love me, her guitar.

When he came out of the bathroom, she was already in bed, her new dress wadded on the coffee table. Sandy fixed two triple gimlets, handing her both while he undressed, his back to her.

What the hell does he think this is, she thinks, a movie?

The light hair along his spine was iridescent in the sunset. He balanced perfectly on one leg as he drew off his trousers by the cuff. She laughed inwardly at his posturing, like a querulous jay strutting and pecking at his reflection in a hubcap, but she also felt that whatever failures were to come would not likely be attributable to him.

In the dresser mirror, the half-light, she blurred as he tried to take her in. With the two gimlets, between the sheets, she looked like a fey scales-of-justice stand-in. As a child, she must have been all eyes; as a crone she would end up all chin. Yet in her present prime she seemed somehow blunted, diffused — like those blocked-out unfinished torsos whose interest derives not from what's been chiseled but from the veil of marble they still carry — a calculated enigma, her face straining through its enviable softness toward character. He felt himself across the chest, sighed silently until the diaphragm relaxed. Then he backed into bed and snapped the sheets over them.

She's nasal, demanding, real wiry; she loves the apartment, exceptionally so. "It's so modern," she says, and her voice shakes like a nineteenth-century Russian narrator. A swimmer once, she explains, which accounts for the hair that tapers like a wood duck at her nape, the freckled solid shoulders, ribs those of a crown roast of lamb, *lattimus dorsi* like the leading edge of a harp, and everything shaved from the eyebrows down, all the ligaments ligature, buttocks like biceps, pigeon toes from which a tendon, a velvet restraining rope, starts on top of her big toe, is strung across the high arch, loops the ankle twice, emerging on the inside of that most interesting muscle of all, the calf, runs on, spirals the knee, then up diagonally across the thigh to the hip's ball joint, then, stringing the telegraph through swamp, peat bogs, hillocks, it splits after steak and spaghetti up each side of the prehistoric spine — ivy, trumpet vine, clematis, the kudzu enveloping the old lichened gatepost where with resignation it attaches its tendrils to the medulla, and from there on it's not felt except when the horses bite.

First they were chaoses; then they were carcasses. Their eyes a single violet transplant between them. She arched and lifted so that his elbows and knees were airbound: *she raised a mortal to the skies/he drew an angel down.* He licked the salt from her ears, the brine from her eyes; the sweat from his brow pooled in her clavicle. Somewhere in the complex, a kitchen exhaust fan and a disposal kicked over. Gradually she ceased to become a blur. Then he was aware of a shape hovering on the edge of his sight, and glanced up to find his own right hand, slung under her neck and reappearing, a jester's claw, above his left ear. "Everywhere," Haas has said, "man meets only himself."

She poked her head out from beneath the blankets, emerging loving and tender, *ad majoram gloriam*. Drawing her clutched thighs along his hip, she kissed him on the chest like a child. Then she looked to him, every feature softened, a slight convulsion in her cheeks, her voice no longer nasal.

"What are you trying to do to me?"

He didn't know what to answer.

She rolled over and spoke sibilantly into the pillows.

"Is it always the same for you?"

"Pretty much. Why not?"

"Why do you do it, then?"

"..."

She barrel-rolled and stared into him.

"I feel you're judging me. That you're...watching me."

"..."

"You make me feel so self-conscious. Don't you know what it's like to feel...taken advantage of...?"

"This talking in bed," Sandy thinks, "this must be something...modern."

But suddenly, she was up in a fury, and stalking to the bathroom she proceeded to dash the three available water tumblers into the basin. The shards exploded about her most impressively. The dull *powp* of distant artillery, the light dry rain from the bunker ceiling. Sandy remained in bed, disconsolate, staring at his long bare feet. She was wailing.

"All you want to do is *fuck* me!"

Sandy pulled the covers over his naked head. She stalked from the bathroom and began to jerk her clothes on as if she were dressing a manikin, cramming her girdle and bra in her purse. Sandy noticed that her legs had begun to go. A new pair of oblate buttocks were beginning to emerge below the originals. A pale network of veins crept down the backs of her thighs, ending in varicose nebulae at the crease of her knees.

She was standing by the window now, hands rammed in her coat pockets.

"Are you using me? Experimenting with me somehow?"

"No."

"Aren't I good for that?"

"Yes."
"Don't you know what you're doing to me?"
"No."
"Don't you really care?"
"Yes."
"For God's sake, do you have to be of two minds about everything? When did *you* get to be *you?*"
"…"
She put her hand to the knob and left with the horsey grin of an unconvincing madwoman.

'All I get,' he thought, 'are heros and victims. Oh Haas!'

It took him most of an hour to sponge up the glass. Then he went out into the sulfurous room and pulled a chair to the window. Rivulets of condensation were forming between the double panes of glass. His legs were blessedly heavy, but he refused to regard himself and resisted sleep. Spying her guitar beneath the coffee table, he opened the fiberboard case and slung it into his lap. It was a commonplace instrument, with some surprisingly fancy inlaid fretwork and the basic fingering positions scratched on the sounding board. He laid his bad hand soundlessly across the gut.

Thursday

The greater the depth of the system, the errors committed early in the calculation are amplified in the latter parts of it, increasing the deterioration of precision...

THE SUN is not yet down, but the wan moon is already on high. Sandy sits in his office sling chair, holding his plug, creating a life all his own. Above him, in the acoustical ceiling, is a grid of black holes in which to place the stars, to separate and adorn the wandering vacancies that mark the festivities and impart a distinctive character to the passing of time. The stars may be replenished or subdued to blur the division between night and day. The ceiling of his office, like his room, is a smudged carbon copy of the heavens; the heavens are a blotted copybook.

He has come off a very hard day with Haas. Watch out when Dr. Haas gets cheerful. Sandy's memory may be imperfect, but Haas is a man who has no history to begin with. His mouth opens deliberately.

"You will be interested to know that this morning I accomplished the equivalent of a 1955 Bank Teller's lifetime work in about 1½ hours."

Sandy feigned a yawn. "Makes you tired, don't it."

"You know, Sandman, pretty soon I'll be Head Honcho. You could move up with me. Not on the technical staff of course. We really need someone to take charge of," his mouth goes sour, "*personnel*. Their lives and things."

"The career will take care of itself, Haas, I've got other things to sort out. You know what I mean."

"Look"—Haas slammed his hand down—"don't you realize what's happening? What we're doing will make the railroad and automobile appear as the merest tertiary ripples on a 500-year wave! Don't you understand? Our lives are going to be changed—radically and irreversibly!"

Sandy leaned back and cracked his knuckles.

"Everybody's telling me that things have got to change, and that we can't do anything about it. It scares the hell out of people, Haas. And to be frank with you, I don't see any change at all. There *may* be larger forces operating—*you* may be able to see something in the pattern—but with people, why, they seem more the same than ever! And, anyway, even if you're right that some of us will survive and some won't, well the feeling out there, in case you don't know it, is that it's a matter of luck, that there's no way you can prepare for it. I couldn't motivate a big yeller dog under these conditions."

"Volatility does not mean chaos," Haas rejoined. "We can *train* cycles. Cycles mean opportunity for those who ride the crests. But you think of change in old-fashioned terms, Boom and Bust, War and Peace. Look at that Memory Drum over there"—the disc's dull whirr accelerated to a whine—"that's *change*. The sound of change. Don't you hear the voices?"

THURSDAY

"Does a bear shit in the woods?"

"Yes, of course," Haas seemed apologetic, "there always seem to be some voices that cannot be eliminated."

"I don't want to listen...to *all* of them! For God's sake, Haas, have pity..."

"Don't be so obtuse. Look, entire civilizations have prospered without religion, without the wheel, without writing, without natural resources, without formal leadership. The only thing that all successful civilizations have in common are *fused metals!* There is matter," Haas mused, sighed, "in the mineral kingdom which is divine."

"So what accounts for their decline? Or is that old hat too?"

"Easy. Every civilization has a secret brotherhood that runs things. They generally have scant respect for human life. Druidical is the model you might say. Consequently, they work people too hard and eventually the people revolt and they are overthrown. The beauty of *our* brotherhood is that our control does not depend on working people to death. Our power is their comfort. In fact, on the whole, we make things easier for them. And when they excavate us, all they'll find are these damn chips — and they'll say, 'Wow, what a civilization!' Because we repeat everything ad nauseum, they'll think we discovered unmistakable cosmic patterns. We will be an open book! No one will know how fickle and cruel and dopey we really were. Yet...everyone will somehow feel our strangeness..."

"You're treating people like children."

"People *want* to be treated like children. And why not?

Children are treated rather well. I ought to know. Because I never was one."

"Oh, Haas." Sandy was mortified.

"Don't get sentimental — you think I'm all brains and no balls. People have a hard time imagining me having sex, don't they?"

"Please, Haas!"

"And don't lay that old authoritarian rap on me. There's nothing secret here. If people want to know how things work they can just walk in and ask. You think they will? Hell, no. They're too lazy. Believe me, Sandy, remember old Haas's basic law: Once people get their hands on the benefits of a technology, they will never be convinced of its detriments until the decision is completely out of their hands!"

Sandy felt that he should appear despondent.

"Look — either it's done this way, or we will have to push people to their genetic limits. We are dealing with a pervasive low-grade infection — pessimism. There's only one way to deal with it — intensify it to a level where the body can reject it."

"So it's a question of joining the brotherhood or not?"

"Don't be a fool. There are checks and balances built into the system just like any other — impedance factors, if you will. The brotherhood is functionally secret — the brothers generally don't know who the other brothers are. They're too busy covering their own asses to mount an effective conspiracy. This is what we call integration…"

"That's evasive."

"No, it's positive. Once any system turns its primary energy

THURSDAY

into investigating itself — its own workings — you're in for trouble. A certain scientific naïveté is necessary for any significant discovery."

Sandy is confused. He doesn't know whether Haas is trying to seduce him or shit on him. He feels like a Skank.

They clearly have suspicious and grudging respect for one another. What is the unspoken part? What is the mean temperature? Why are the horses standing at the door?

Before Haas left he gave Sandy a practice problem to storify, some Skank's accounting he had bought for a song, filed under *The Seduction of Tommy G.*, which Sandy dutifully encoded.

6/15	Tommy G., Chris and Margery. Beef ragout. spinach salad. rice. cheese cake.
7/4	Felice-Bud. Marion-Phillip. Tommy G. Shrimp dish. string beans. strawberry shortcake.
7/21	Jackie-Mark. Rita-Orin. Tommy G. Flank steak oriental. broccoli. pita bread. mousse.
8/5	Gerard. Flank steak oriental. cheese cake.
8/20	Marilee-Tommy G., Gerard. Chicken and dumplings. spinach salad. chocolate chip something.
8/30	Tommy G., Rudy-Lisa. Turkey casserole. carrot ring. brownie.
9/7	Tommy G., Robbie-Chuck. Flank steak oriental. noodle pudding.
9/8	Tommy G., 2 poached eggs. English muffins. strawberry yogurt.

WHITE JAZZ

Bleary-eyed, he pushed the storification button, and the printout was in his hands momentarily.

THE SEDUCTION OF TOMMY G.
(1st storification)

Incidental Music	Specially composed and recorded	$16,000
Props and Costumes	Estimate	$64,000
Legal Services	Estimate	$13,000
Camera Depreciation	1 Steadicam w/CP-16 and zoom @ $3,600/day	$36,000
	1 CP-16 w/zoom & mags & tripod @ $1,350/day	$ 6,750
Sound Equipment Depreciation		$ 1,840
Lights	Estimate	$ 4,000
Phone Costs	Estimate	$ 2,000
Photocopying	Estimate	$ 1,000
Film Processing (Chemtone Process)	220,000 ft. @ $.084/ft.	$10,848
Workprinting	220,000 ft. @ $.141/ft.	$30,102
Sound Transfers	$35/hr. for 120 hrs.	$ 4,200
Animation Photography		$ 1,500
Titles		$20,500
Conforming Original		$10,000
Sound Mix	$160/hr. plus $400 for 35mm full coat and lab charges	$20,320
Optical Transfer	20,200 ft. @ $.115/ft.	$ 2,530
Magnetic Transfer	Estimate	$ 1,800
Effects	Estimate	$ 4,000
ABC Answer Print	20,200 ft. @ $.275/ft.	$ 6,050
2nd Answer Print	20,200 ft. @ $.21/ft.	$ 4,620
CRI	20,200 ft. @ $.8363/ft.	$10,840
Check Print	20,200 ft. @ $.17/ft.	$ 3,740
4 Release Prints	80,800 ft. @ $.1186/ft.	$10,044
	Total	$285,684

THURSDAY

The sling chair has become a web. In a dim way Sandy is now hyperactive, passively frustrated. His sinuses are tentacles. His brain is Cordon Bleu. He is aware that he is not in control. Someone has taken time out. They are in a holding pattern. Cross-processing is inhibited. He is nationwide and one, but dimmed and unwhole at the same moment. He senses that he is deprived and not unique for this; that he can will neither intimacy nor distance. Only put the stars in their predrilled holes.

In his course catalogue he checks off the academic requirements he has managed to avoid so far: "Properties Defined by Forbidden Subroutines," "Minimalization of Transmission on Optimal Rendezvous," "Estimation as an Inverse Problem," and the ball breaker, "A Scattering Theory Framework for Recursive Smoothing of Deterministic Data." He calculates that he only has one elective left, and notes that for the next term there is a new course offering: *Horticultural Therapy 762,* "...soothing work with exotic material, feel the power of propagation, self-image and esteem raised by accord accredited status of peers and counselors, aggression lowered...."

Holding his plug, Sandy writes in his journal. "What happens to aggression that is lowered? Is it rechanneled, recycled, or displaced? Can it be leached out of the garden?" Professor Jordan would go for that.

Professor Bob Jordan taught the Humanities requirement at the Community College. He was quite old, very old, older than he looked even, utterly white-haired and bearded, once a very large and active man apparently, to judge from his bone structure, limp, and numerous scars. As well as the occasional inappropriate boyishness. He was teaching past retirement because he had no pension, as he constantly reminded them in a spare monosyllabic monotone, the simplicity of which was highly mannered.

Sandy is Professor Jordan's favorite student because he is the only one who can pronounce Diderot properly. "Why, Professor Jordan, why when I drive to work each morning do I encounter no ennobling images to uplift mine heart or even beat it off? All I see are grotesquely fat cowboys, bearded legendary figures from our bearded unlegendary past, and pigs, mice, horses, birds that would embarrass a dog, I'll tell you, all nature pantalooned and begloved — why, Professor, they're not *that* cute, these animals; what does this have to do with *us,* especially when we're simply on our way down the road to diagram our interpersonal sentences? It's just not the food, Professor; we can take the food. It's possible that we can take anything! Except these animations of ourselves. They may be very sharp and all, but they don't have all their fingers, these figures. All brains and talk and plots and personality but no history or genitalia. They should be in the Government or something, not just beckoning to us out there, celebrating our most habitual and banal functions. What lovers should never have to know is up there on those signs!"

He had asked Haas first about the animals. "It's because they're lovelier, of course," he said, a new keloidal pustule glowing on the very tip of his nose, "It's because most people are unspeakably ugly."

THURSDAY

Wanda June pointed out that in fairy tales, men and friendly animals cooperate in the task at hand. It was some kind of forgotten alliance.

Entelechy was a bit taken aback but speculated that their costumes were necessary as each act of intercourse left horrible traces on their bodies.

The Professor was more theoretical when he took him aside. "It's the natural process of democracy, son, to represent something intrinsically grotesque as sweet and capable of entertainment... but you err when you believe them to be intimations of *us*. These are the modern cherubim, a divine security force that guards the way to the Tree of Life."

When Sandy reported the Professor's interpretation back to Haas to complete the circle, he was only faintly amused. "Well, they may not be of our dominion, but those ruddy cheerful countenances will be *ours* on the last day. For each idle and useless idea we have, God sends us one of these florid angel babies, sort of his way of keeping count. They get furrier as we age, and eventually they take up most of the picture. Think of it as a crowding out."

At home, on the ARTS Channel, the Hispanic is ranting again, "*¡Rabiosamente, compañeros! Somos en un desmoronamiento continuo.*" [We are in a continual disintegration.]

Sandy finds when he touches the TV, the picture becomes less jittery. He is a rectifier.

"*¿Vamos a terminar nuestras querellas?*" [Let's bury the hatchet, eh?]

Tonight the classroom smells like a new car. The seminar table is simulated rosewood. The chairs are airliner swivel recliners with infinitely adjustable lumbar support. The lights are recessed and the cement-block walls are painted a comforting beige, with lime polyurethane trim, easy on the eyes. All audiovisual equipment is hidden for the day, panels are down, flaps enfolded, lenses shuttered, speakers recessed and stuffed with Handi-Wipes.

The class swivels, snivels, swivels, making infinite adjustments to its quite individualistic postures. Professor Jordan enters angrily. He has a sheaf of last week's essays under his arm, and despite the protest of the young lady who has paid her good money for a dialogue, he lectures them, scratching definitions on the green blackboard, slivering the spines of his words with the screeches of chalk, breaking up their cursive note-taking with his tax-dollar-supported cynicism.

"Do not do this to me again," he says. "It is not that you are improficient or unself-disciplined or lack self-expression, but this work is airless; it lacks point of view and conviction and bold characterization, narrative momentum, verisimilitude, and corroborative detail, compassion, endurance, and prevelation!"

He had an odd way of teaching literature, of seeing things in books that weren't there. They were doing Hemingway that week. It was not a good week. But as good a week as you could expect. They always ruined it somehow. They always ruined the good weeks in the end. Usually by Thursday.

Professor Jordan asked a question:

"Why doesn't Nick Adams fish the swamp at the end of the Big Two-Hearted River?"

"He's already got two fish?"

"No."

"He knows that if he goes over the limit some day there won't be any fish left?"

"No."

"He's hungry and it's getting dark?"

"No."

Sandy raised his hand. "I think...he misses his father...."

"Um," Professor Jordan said, "now we're getting someplace. There's a theme there, isn't there?"

"He's afraid," Sandy went on, "he will end up like his father."

The Professor shook his head. "It doesn't say that anywhere, sonny boy."

"Like his father," Sandy persevered, "in the swamp."

"Close enough. If you can't prove something, write it down," Professor Jordan said. "Write it down as a fine experience. Let's break for five minutes."

This was the way things had gone. He always got you in the end, no matter how perceptive you were. The sky was dark, and the wind was warm on Sandy's shoulders. At the *Laughing Turtle,* before class, the turtle was sitting upright, flippers across his chest, in the fey manner of multiple sclerosis. This turtle had on spats and a Greek fisherman's hat, and from his beak there issued a soundless apoplectic roar. The pompano was dry and flat but the baked potato was delish. This was the week from whom the bells toll.

"*Salud,*" the Professor said, as he returned from the washroom. "Let us get on with it."

"I'm tired," a girl yawned. "I been on my feet all day."

"We should continue," the Professor said.

"It's been a terrible day! Do you know what it is to work *all* day?" the girl went on.

"We will rest at the finish," Professor Bob Jordan said.

Professor Bob had a surprise for them. He pulled down what was presumed to be a map of the world or perhaps a chart of the elements, but it was a movie screen. They were going to see the movie of the book and compare *genres,* Professor Bob said. This seemed to calm the class.

Sandy wasn't prepared for this. He had trouble identifying with Gary Cooper, but he sure did like that young Ingrid Bergman. At the very moment Ingrid Bergman was grabbing phantom cock in a sleeping bag, *El Cielito Lindo*'s doors were opening and Maestro Luncheon would be reigning over the cereal monogamy, it was truly wonderful to watch Ingrid Bergman squint her gray eyes and brush her cropped hair.

When the lights came back on and the class rubbed their eyes, Sandy was never more agitated.

"Well?" Professor Jordan said.

"Oh shit," Sandy exclaimed, "what a stupid ending!"

He looked around for support from the class but could adduce nothing but minor apathy and middling terror. "But Ingrid Bergman. How could he let Ingrid Bergman go!" Sandy was shouting. The Professor was grimacing and gritting his teeth.

"He must stay. He hates to leave her. But he must stay," the Professor insisted.

"That's ridiculous. He can hold them off for a while and then catch up. All the probabilities are in his favor..."

Professor Bob stared balefully at the class.

"The leg it is broken. The big nerve is hurting. Such swelling!"

"For Christ's sake. You're not going to let Ingrid Bergman get away because your frigging leg's broke. It's not even a compound fracture!"

"The bone, it is in the muscle," Professor Bob Jordon whined.

"So you're gonna let *her* get away because of a lousy hematoma? You know what? I figured it all out. It ends like that because he didn't want a happy ending. That's all. Either that or he wants to die. He's got *half an hour* by his own admission. He wants some fucking bullshit *tragic adventure,* that's what!"

The Professor drew himself to his actual height. "Well, son, I suppose you could do it better?"

"I can tell you what the right end would be." Sandy swiveled, breathless. "This asshole does try to shoot the Fascists as they go by, but just like he forgot his brandy flask to kill the pain, he forgot his gun grease, too, and the gun jams so he can't kill 'em. So he's just there, see, this guerrilla guy, helpless, the Fascists are in this big hurry, so he lays low until some Republicans find him and set the leg—you know, with old sticks or something. No problema! Jesus, Professor, Art Entelechy once played half a football game with a broken leg! Anyway, he meets back up with Maria in Madrid and marries her like he said he would 'cause it was his duty, and a kid is born and lives this time; he remembers to tip the doctors this time; and they live well and cheaply in Spain till Franco wins — why do they call themselves *Republicans,* anyway? — and then they go to Gibraltar when the war starts and he's drafted and he's put to work translating artillery manuals into Spanish and because of his involvement with the Pinkos, he can't get security clearance and they live on an air base in the English midlands for the duration, where Maria has the flu all the time and runs at both ends and the earth no longer moves when they do it, even the mattress no longer moves when they do it, and Maria, like many women of Iberia, gets pretty fat pretty young, and the kid is lovely in his way but he's also dumb and ugly, as peasant stock often is, if he was wire-haired and could hunt on all fours he would be a lot happier...at sixteen, when his father's sixty, that boy's going to be doing a lot of walking around kicking tires and spitting in the street, you know...and after the war's over he returns to his alma mater to teach two sections of intermediate Spanish for beginners and three sections of freshmen comp, and they no longer have servants, her relatives in Barcelona write Maria that the younger generation is fucking their brains out, and Maria gets fatter and fatter and sleeps with the Puerto Rican who delivers the dry cleaning, and he gets softer and his cheeks get rounder and finally he doesn't get tenure because between 1938 and 1949 he has published only the complete artillery manuals of the Spanish Republican Cavalry, and Maria's English is no

THURSDAY

longer funny and the kid is dyslexic, so he runs off with a graduate student who in fact does restore him for a time...until his salary is attached in an alimony decision; the lawyer for Maria gives fee-free assistance to wives of veterans of the Spanish Civil War and the grad student discovers she can earn $18.50 an hour working for Delta, with unlimited travel benefits, and leaves him...he develops bursitis, sinusitis, pancreatitis, and spends the rest of his life teaching Spanish to ignorant Americans, English to ignorant spics in an interdisciplinary college close to the expressway — now there's a *tragic* adventure for you, maybe that's why he doesn't want to go into the swamp, sir..."

Professor Bob Jordan had become strangely ecstatic.

"Yes, yes! That's what I've been trying to get through to you all, all along. Life *does* go on when the book ends, doesn't it? Words stuffed into our mouths, our little destinies forced upon us by somebody's notion of what's shapely? No you can't buffalo old Bob Jordan. You live in the most interesting of times, my young friends. I know what it's like to live in the most interesting of times — it's not easy — and how necessary it is to hold the secrets of the age to your breast, to withhold information lest you be betrayed. I know that you have tales of power locked within you, your fascinating perishable lives larded with emotional crises so profound as to put a poet out of business, despair and thrills are your everyday lot; so I say, listen to your people! Graph their heartaches, capture their speech, reveal their innermost thoughts; there are a million stories out there between every man and every woman; don't be tricky, don't be cute, bring those stories in dead or alive; give us all a break!"

Sandy scribbles furiously in his journal, holding his pud; he realizes you can't both type and hold your pud, that is the secret of the scribe, as Professor Jordan adumbrates another line of inquiry — i.e., that eroticism is a notoriously slippery foundation on which to base a society already in a sea change...he rails against those minds that think against themselves, those who refuse to acknowledge what is *most human* about men and women, though this he does not specify, those artists who reflect only on the despair and alienation of their age; sickness is an old-fashioned idea, he goes on, everyone knows that even in this country life is more rich, more varied, more frangible than these nasty brutish caricatures, these puppets who are trotted out to demean us all...let us have stories worthy of us, not these surreal anti-life easy ironies, these pessimistic abortions, and as you leave this class, open your eyes and your feelings so that your great humanity and the beauty of the world may not be lost on you...it is for you, bright youths, that these doors were opened: enter the armory and equip thyselves!

The night class disperses into the night. Sandy calculates that over the last hour he has completed an additional 0.16 of a credit toward his M.A., which, prorated over a lifetime, has just increased his aggregate earning power by $1.52 in nonadjusted dollars.

Sandy is beguiled, light-headed in fact. He will walk home; fuck the Pontiac. The night is clear and warm, and the stars, if not bright precisely, are well lit through the clouds of exhaust. He strides purposefully across the vastness of the empty parking lot. The Pontiac is as lonely as the last pear of winter. He looks

THURSDAY

down at the intersection from a balustrade, down through the interstices of light. Professor Bob Jordan is right. There *is* more out here than is commonly told. What might look like robotic rodents to a diseased and cynical mind during the hard press of the day, are more like...molecules and atoms, more like, yes, fallen stars in a way. He makes a ring of his forefinger and thumb, encircles the taillight of a passing truck, gradually enclosing the finger ring until the agate is extinguished; then, looking to the heavens, he performs the same sensuous trick upon the North Star and finally upon the moon. His sinuses flush. Eyebrows knot in pain. Could it be the moon and not the cathode rays that is accountable for his allergies? Is the moon Bad Light? There would be more precedent, more recursive data, for the moon, certainly. Dr. Onarga's old question: Does the allergy generate internally or emanate from the world? Haas's point is the pain is equivalent whichever theory you prefer. The equivalence of pain is what keeps the music going.

The headlights weave, the phosphors glow. Sandy tries to ingest the light. In his office with his console, things seem clearer, not only easier to follow, but clearer. Out here there seems to be a film between Sandy and the lights, a film that is more than smog. He would trade off acuity for relief from the pain. Haas is right again. There *is* something, some kind of befouled tissue, some Third Eye, out there between him and the world...How he envies the truckers, the only ones without hard-ons, their parts softened by fatigue and the vibrations of the felt life, their inflation-proof wage pacts, kidneys eventually moussed by their eternal partings....

Then, it seems, the bridge exploded. Just like it did in the movie except that this burst of flame hurt Sandy's eyes terribly. The tissue, for an instant, was gone. The pain, for an instant, was gone. He made his way cautiously down the median strip, between the stinking ginkgos and honey locusts, the lanes now slowly clotting with irritated, unsuspecting traffic. Blue, green, and red strobes, indifferent sirens, approached from every direction. Apparently an ammonia truck had come off the ramp too fast, struck the guard rail, the tanker plunging off the bridge onto a gaggle of autos, while the cab remained snarled in the railing of the overpass. The ammonia was burning furiously, a pool of flame covered all eight lanes, the pin oaks were alight in one of the cloverleafs like a Hanukkah candelabrum, and at least a hundred cars lay about in various stages of wounded and maimed desuetude. A police helicopter held the wreckage in its nacreous searchlights, the eighteen-wheeler tank strung detumescent from the overpass to the flaming superslab beneath.

Above this chasm the *El Cielito Lindo*'s sign turned slowly in the malillumination and Sandy could hear *The Conquerors'* chorus drifting above the screams and the honks....

> *Ai, yi, yi-yi*
> *come to your window....*

All in all, it was a great signature scene.

Returning to the Pontiac, he switches on the CB, always in hopes that overhearing a conversation will change his life, that somehow there *is* a secret, any secret, out there.

THURSDAY

Hey there, Beaver Lady, I got an eyeball on your seat covers down there, but I can't get through. Everybody must be walkin' the dog. Threes on you.

It's your nickel, good buddy. You're wall to wall and walkin' tall, but you're whompin' on me, and I'm gone.

Mercy me and great day there, Beaver Lady, why you gettin' off at Exit 9?

Well, we kinder live here on Exit 9, Bucketmouth.

Well, hang my needle. Clear there with you, young lady. What's your handle anyways?

This be The Dreamer, Struttin'-Style. We clear. We down. We gone. We out!

Well then, Dreamer, have a good day today. And a better one tomorrow.

It was four hours before Sandy was permitted to cross the overpass, and by then even *El Cielito Lindo* had closed down. He saw how Professor Bob must have felt when he blew his bridge, how nothing since could be equal to it. Maybe he had better look into that *Horticultural Therapy*. This Humanities stuff was dangerous. Disaster, once the province of the skilled and dedicated professional, was now the prerogative of anyone capable of a single moment of inattention. To stop the music, all you had to do was...close your eyes and keep the pedal to the floor...oh, what a single troubled man can do!...

The stars seem to be closing in, a curtain opalescing its own reflection. Sandy is constricted in his room, the grid of black holes above him are imploding, and for the first time in years, against his best impulses, he furiously masturbates. Amen, Amen.

Friday

The perpetuating properties of the genes can apparently relocate, leak as it were, outside the genes, into the remaining portion of the cell...

THE SKY swarms with snow geese, brant, and canvasback driven in from the coast by a hurricane. The drainage ditches roil with spawning catfish and unlikely snook following the newly brackish waters. Despite high winds, amphibious carp have been sighted off the coast, frolicking, leaping in heavy foam-flecked seas, just waiting for the tides that will provide access to cistern, septictank, and swimming pools. Mongrel bitches drag their tied mates upside down bemused and backward through the alleys, and the cattle are, well, lowing.

This is the afternoon Sandy has been waiting for all week, for the time is right to reconstruct an algorithm of Tyler's and Travis's early life together, to resynchronize that series of deflections of which Sandy can barely recall — only that it seemed so happy and promising, at least for him. His suspicion has always been that they gave up their happiness, their own and everyone else's, for him. Which would have been all right had the world as well as their only son been better than they were.

WHITE JAZZ

The data breakthrough had come in the Vacation file and the bills. It seemed that Tyler had kept every bill for forty years, in perpetual justifiable fear of audit. The Accounts Receivable graphed an ascending exponential curve of consumption and expended energy astounding in its arc, and Sandy realized that if indeed he was heir to this progression, he was already off the paper, plotted beyond the frame. He would never be equal it.

Sandy has taken Haas's advice; he has suspended disbelief, he has formalized his discourse. This once, he will not try the cumulative existing programs. He will let the Third Eye do its business.

His attention, as always, is to one great question: How Did They Fly the Distance?

He logs into the software, settles back in his chair. The storification has begun.

Art Alarum

No joke. Tyler and Travis now have separate bedrooms. No problem, as there are four nice ones still available. Still the smallest in the family, Sandy retains the least large room, the one with the radiator that flakes toxic lead paint and the ridiculous closet space. Tyler, taller, uses the master one, the king-sized mattress with the bloodstains and the French wallpaper stippled with blue paisley. An octagonal bay gives out on the yard, his prerogative. Travis has bought herself a cannonball bed with an extra-firm mattress for her slight and delightful curvature of the spine, as well as an Empire campaign desk and dresser ensemble. The peasant curtains clash with the pointillist wallpaper, but what the hell, it's Travis's first private room since she was nine. She has even more magazines now than then.

The remaining room has been designated an office/guest room, tax write-off. But there will be no guests for a while. Since their crisis, these two are on bad terms with their respective families and friends. And that is somehow more painful than their own estrangement: that perfect word. Tyler and Travis are both thirty-one now, and this first shared crisis of their ten-year marriage, through which Sandy has been with them from the beginning. There will be other crises, at forty-four and fifty-seven — the first related to Tyler's career, the second to Travis's glands — and of course it will also be difficult when Sandy goes. But this foreknowledge which they know makes their species unique, does not suffice.

Their friends speculate about this attractive couple, universally admired for their refusal to offer advice or confess a thing. The diagnoses fall short of the mark. Travis refuses to see a shrink because she knows she is smarter than they are, and Tyler openly concurs with this. With the oblique masculine, he assumes that he is the cause of her problem and must bear with it. One thing, though, is that Tyler, once quite competitive, all elbows and knees, has come to love practically everyone quite fiercely, except Travis, while Travis, once so open and charming, a real credit, has begun to moon and bark. She even accuses Tyler of fucking on the side, which he wishes were true and thus cannot convincingly refute.

With Tyler, it isn't a question of starting over. He's not mad *about* anyone else. He's no longer even mad *at* Travis. Even when, like the other night, she lay groveling, sobbing at the bottom of the stairs while Tyler drank in the tax write-off, grinding his teeth, thinking that as long as he wasn't going to leave Travis, he'd be damned if he'd have to go downstairs. Their friends felt sorry for Travis feeling so sorry for herself, and sorry for Tyler because he had never been allowed to feel sorry for himself.

Tyler's trees were in trouble too. Tyler owned two of the largest elms in Elm City, trees more than four hundred years old. In the summer, they threw a canopy over the entire lot. In the winter, they held tons of snow in their massive crotches. Tyler could sit in the tax write-off and watch them for hours. Those anaconda limbs dwarfed even the pink sun as it slid through them. And at sunset Tyler would always do some figuring: let's see, the sun's 2,000,000,000, the trees are 400, the country's 201, the state, uh, 102, the town 50-some, we're 31. Sandy will be 10 in March, and the cannonball bed is about 1 week now....Dutch elm was ravaging Elm City.

Travis despised the trees in particular, though in general she knew that Elm City wouldn't be the same without them. She had seen pictures of neighboring towns after the chestnut blight, real nice respectable towns like Elm City, which suddenly looked as common without the trees as some Nebraska burg. But Travis hated the way the trees hung over the house...if even a small limb should fall?...The roots pressed against the basement walls causing them to sweat; they slurped up water and fertilizer that was meant for the mock orange, no grass or garden would grow beneath them, and the few seedlings that Travis managed to start in the interstices of sunlight that the limbs permitted were soon trampled by Sandy and his friends. Pansy, hibiscus, rose of Sharon—which, when Travis's mother grew them, were as large as softballs split at the seams after lying in a rainy outfield for a month—were unknown here, and even the Miracle Shrub, which the catalogue said would be resplendent with immense white flowerets all summer, luscious purple berries in the fall, colorful red bark in the winter, and cream and lime variegated foliage to fool the spring forsythia, never legally died but took no notice of the seasons. "Bloom," boomed Tyler, "bloom, you bastards!" A lot he knew. The poppies he claimed he ordered never arrived.

What had arrived was the arborist. Tyler cringed in the tax write-off with Sandy. Travis met the man civilly at the door but made him wait outside. Then she knocked on Tyler's door. "Jesus, Tyler," she said, "the arborist's southern. His name is Fondue Reedy, or something like that."

Tyler finished his beer, and after a limp handshake took the arborist out to the trees. He seemed quite soft for a tree-man, a moon of a red face and bell-bottomed denims. Over his left army shirt pocket was a faded rectangle where his military name had been.

Tyler hugged the largest of the elms, his long thin arms reaching not even a quarter of the circumference, wedging his loafers between the roots.

"You think it's got it?"

Fondue stared upward where Tyler was pointing: a large lower branch with a lemony hue.

"If'n it don't, it's a pretty good imitation."

"We've had a cold summer..." Tyler began hopelessly.

"If'n it don't come down by me, the city'll take it. Just a matter of time. Suit up yerself."

"Have you seen any elms this big in town?" Tyler stalled.

"Not standin'."

Tyler peered at the man.

"You want some recommendations, mister?"

"No...no." Tyler was distracted. "Well, how much to take them down?"

"One grand per gentleman."

"Isn't that an awful lot?"

"I'm not gonna wampus around up in that gentleman for the love of it, mister."

"Well, I didn't expect..."

"Hold yer taters, mister. You know what I got to do? I got to top that gentleman if it don't flip my ass across this county. Then I got to drop it so it don't fall on your garage or on that power line. Then I got to cut the son of a bitch up into two-, three-foot pieces, then I got to truck 'em fifty miles to the burnin' place, then I got to bring that truck back empty. We all got problems. I'd only do for you what I'd do for myself."

"There's no way to save them?"

"Yeah, there's stuff. I injected a hunnert trees with it in Tennessee. But it ain't been governmint tested yet. It's a hunch, that's all."

"How much for that?"

"Five taters per diameter inch. No guarantee."

FRIDAY

"What do you think, though?"

"Wal, a grand's worth eleven hunnert, mister."

"All right, Mr. Reedy, let's take a good swing at the pitch." And Tyler shook hands and turned rapidly toward the house.

"In the mornin' if nothin' don't happen."

As soon as the arborist had left, Tyler looked outside to check the yellowness. It seemed to have spread an inch or so since Fondue Reedy had left, and if he couldn't arrest it, the city inspector would spot it for sure. They had taken down all the elms along the parkway only three blocks from Tyler in the last week. He looked at the trails and favorite hiding places Sandy had made in the privet hedge, and then he glanced up at Travis's room where the shades were drawn. Tyler picked up the newspaper, which was so wet it disintegrated in his hands. Sandy charged by him and into the house, where he threw himself mewling on the sofa. A short and sudden peace descended on Tyler, which made him very itchy.

Travis had been watching Tyler from the small slits, made with cuticle scissors, in the shades of her new own room. Beyond him, she could see the neighbor lady, Ricki, already at work in her new Spanish Provincial kitchen. The neighbors, Ricki and Franklin, were Travis's and Tyler's best friends. Franklin worked with Tyler at the office, where they respected one another. Until recently, Travis and Ricki talked about everything and shared their problems. Once Ricki had even taken Travis to a group where they were to "act out their problems," but despite a good deal of crying and kissing and hugging, it depressed Travis

WHITE JAZZ

more than not. Just as Tyler felt responsible for his failure with Travis, Travis felt responsible for her inability to respond to the group. Ricki had perhaps compounded the problem by suggesting in the group that Travis's problem might be her relationship with Sandy. "He obeys me, but he won't play with me," Travis explained. The group suspected Travis was not telling the whole truth, that if she were more honest with herself, and open with them, she might be able to put things in perspective. "But I *am* being honest and open," she insisted. "Tyler doesn't love me as much as I want him to. What could be more honest and open than that?" One of the women began to stroke her soothingly. "Please," whimpered Travis, "don't... Maybe I just need something better than the truth."

Later on, Ricki suggested that it might be fun if the two couples all had sex together. "You can love more than one person," she said.

"Maybe," said Travis, "but what if they all don't love you?"

"We all love each other, don't we?" Ricki said.

When Travis asked Tyler about this, he was of the opinion that it would complicate his relationship with Franklin. "I need a good accountant more than I need to get laid," he said. Travis agreed for once.

To tell the truth, Tyler had had sex with Ricki once, a long time ago. He had been weeding under her kitchen window, having begged off golf with Franklin, and Ricki had invited him in for some coffee. Ricki had no furniture in her living room then except enormous vinyl-covered beanbags. She lay down on one, and asked Tyler if he wanted to have sex. Before they did, Ricki

FRIDAY

put on a pair of earphones and turned the stereo up. Tyler wondered what she was listening to, and envied Franklin out there duffing around.

Afterward, Tyler went back home and urinated, spattering the toilet seat and shag rug. Later, in the tax write-off, he could hear Travis muttering "Pig, pig," as she cleaned up after him.

That evening, after taking his turn putting Sandy to bed and having a few drinks, Tyler knocked on Travis's door to say good night and serve her the summary of a TV show that he had digested intermittently between chores.

"There were these three couples, you see, and the emcee sends the wives out and tells the husbands to draw pictures of their wives in their most characteristic activities. They give them easels, and one does his wife on the phone, another does her washing and drying, and the third wife, I think, was taking a nap. None of the wives, when they came back on stage, could guess which drawing was of her. Of course, they weren't very good drawings. How do you think I would draw you, Travis? What would you be doing?"

Travis didn't answer directly but gave Tyler a summary of the evening news. Verisimilitude she had, perhaps, but her sadness lacked something.

Fondue Reedy arrived just before noon. The family dog toddled out to greet him but cowered when he saw the unnamable tools. Fondue had brought his club-cab pickup with two 500-gallon drums and two silent, surly helpers of rusticated mountainous origin. These two began to drill holes in the ground at the perimeter of the front elm's drip line, while Fondue began to pump the contents of the two drums into the holes. Then Fondue jerked himself up the trunk with a lineman's belt and boot spikes. Just below the primary crotch, he drilled into the trunk and inserted two pipes, which even before he descended, began to drip an opaque froth.

"What's the idea here?" Tyler asked.

"Ain't no fact of the matter, mister, just something in my head. When somethin's goin to bad, you use what medercine you got."

"It doesn't sound very scientific," Tyler said.

"The wife wants me to get out of this line of work," Fondue replied.

Then he looked up into the great web of branches, feigning an admiring squint.

"Can't get m'belt around her," Fondue went on, "she's so wide around, and you know what, mister, she gets thicker as she goes. I never hardly saw a tree like that." Then he grinned for the first time. "Sure would like to have a woman like that."

The comparison puzzled Tyler. "I don't see why..." he began.

Fondue turned quickly. And Tyler could see that below the soft face, Fondue's neck cords were as thick as his fingers. And that his fingers had the texture and diameter of seaman's rope. In fact, Fondue was the only man Tyler ever saw whose forearms were larger than his biceps and calves, and whose trapezius, thumbs, wrists, dick, and ears appeared to be of equal weight.

"Say," Fondue said softly, slowly, neck cords still pulsating, "when I was up in that there tree, I saw a lady lookin at me from the winder. Is that your wife anyway?"

"Of course."

"Boy, oh, boy. You sure got yourself a pill there. A real lemon…"

Tyler was so taken aback that absolutely nothing occurred to him, even astonishment. But Fondue had already turned away and, dropping his useless safety belt to the ground, began again to climb the elm, chain saw dangling from a cord about his wrist.

As many times as Tyler had stared up into that tree he had not absorbed its enormity until he saw Fondue dwarfed in its crown. The arborist moved gingerly toward the diseased limb, jerked the saw into a whine, and the yellowness shuddered just before the limb crashed with tremendous force into the lawn. Tyler cursed in delayed action; he saw the leaves crackle where Fondue was and then an odd flash of light. The two helpers were staring openmouthed, rubbernecked; Tyler could hear the dog running in nervous circles behind him. Then Tyler saw the chain saw hurtling in the sunlight, but even before it disappeared into the privet hedge, he was aware of Fondue's crumpled body on the sidewalk not five feet from him.

The scream of the chain saw assumed a more human tone as the two helpers ran for the truck. Tyler stared incredulously as they peeled away, though it was true that incredulity always seemed to relax Tyler. He stepped over Fondue's body, strangely unbloody, reminding Tyler somehow of a documentary he had once seen on elk hunting in Manitoba. The chain saw had ceased its chattering in the privet, and Tyler regarded the severed limb, its yellowness now more menacing than ever, sunken in the lime-green turf. And then glancing up, he saw Travis's face, impassive at the window of her room. Her long black hair was spread over her shoulders where she had been brushing it, and in her right hand she held an oval hand mirror. Tyler carried the trembling pup into the house, propped him up in an easy chair, wiped his nose and eyes, and, after a few soothing words, turned on the Auburn-Missouri game.

After the police and doctors and reporters and lawyers had milled around the front yard for a while, Tyler came out on the front steps to answer any questions, which weren't all that tough. Travis gave Sandy his dinner and put him to bed. Their friends, the neighbors, were there. Franklin staring puzzled at the corpse, and when Travis suddenly appeared on the front porch in a dashing matador pantsuit, Ricki embraced her and Travis began to weep and shake. When the men turned Fondue over, everybody looked up into the elm, many perhaps for the first time in their lives, far more than just a glance, except one man who was entranced with the torn end of the fallen limb. He touched it, smelled of it, and then walked slowly to each of the large trees, marking them 823 and 824 respectively with an aerosol paint can.

Ricki was hugger-muggering Travis. Tyler stood up straight

and felt his underchin unfold. Ricki took Travis home to listen to some stereo.

A week later, Tyler got a notice from Elm City Hall that he had two weeks to get the two elms down or they'd slap a tax lien on him, and take them down themselves in the public interest.

On the pretext of saving his marriage, Tyler arranged for a Caribbean vacation.

The air approach to the island was disappointing. A green puddle in the blue slough. As they disembarked from their aircraft, Tyler and Travis sported identical white linen suits and madras ties, matching attaché case and sling bag in moroccan leather. Ricki had offered to take care of Sandy and the pup. The island was overine with karate-type waves on one side and a hotel strip on the smooth and tepid lee.

Travis loved the sun and the change of routine, and took long afternoon naps in a hammock, the first time she had slept during the day since she was nine. A quick tan brought out the beauty of her bones, but as much as Tyler enjoyed Travis's new health, he was never more bored.

"The Iowa of oceans," he grumbled into the flat wavelets which lapped into the lagoon whenever Tyler looked up. There were no sunsets, much less anything to frame them. At five-fifty every day the equatorial red sun fell quite suddenly into the sea like a spangle into dishwater. Floating face down with his disgusting snorkel, Tyler traded glares with the jellyfish and coral bunnies, wondering if regarding them was the point.

The fishing was ridiculously straightforward: You simply threw some barracuda bait from a boat and five minutes later horsed in an enormous grouper or something of the *genre* and watched the natives hit it on the head with an oar. The dolphin fish, iridescent in their element, turned a Dutch elm color upon being horsed over the gunwales. On the fo'c'sle, expiring in the heat, trickles of black blood from the corner of its parrot mouth, a blue marlin stared Tyler down. And as they made for home, its great sail gradually retracted into its body, and the golden iris turned green and then extinguished altogether. 'So that's what happens to you,' Tyler thought.

Tyler generally took his laps in the saltwater pool where he could at least count how far he swam. But one day he swam out to a small, classy yacht anchored in the lagoon and was welcomed aboard by the owners, a retired plastics executive and his kind-of-wife, who explained to him the joys of the simple life. Looking around the tiny galley with all the instrumentation, Tyler was once again incredulous — driving that thing around the ocean would be like commuting to work in a VW in the midst of a truck convoy while watching a test pattern on TV and listening to Officer Bob with the weather report over and over. If that was retirement, he thought, he'd rather work until he toppled over at his desk with thundering apoplexy.

Even the predictable soporific climate gave Tyler no solace: indeed, the entire idea of the equator struck him as absurd. It reminded him of having sex with Ricki with earphones in the beanbag. He'd rather have Travis snoring softly through the wall.

FRIDAY

their vast silences over dinner, than the whole damn archipelago.

Worst of all, Tyler was taller than any tree on the entire island. And when he looked out on the horizon and saw a tanker, all he could think of was how his house would look without the trees when they got back: just like that tanker, a stupid rusted rectangle in a larger prison of air.

The one thing Tyler did like was lying on his back in the sand — not the actual warmth and certainly not the leisure which afforded Travis so much pleasure, but simply the illuminated tissue of his eyelids, a night watch in daylight, blood pumping through the fine capillaries, bacteria slobbering discreetly on his retinas.

If Travis was in her element, Tyler was already converting it to energy. The only way he could deal with it.

They accompany their matching outfits to dinner, the first to act on the gong struck by an uncompromising Mayan. The natives think *they* are handsome; *they* think the natives beautiful. And the word is passed, on both sides: "Behave." Tyler's hand, reaching for a corn chip to do the dip into pummeled avocado, is gray beneath the mosquito-warding lights. My hand, he thinks, is not actually gray.

Through mutual admiration, they are given the best table at the edge of the parapet where the lagoon and the angelfish slop just six feet below. Travis X's their window on a picture postcard of the hotel to send off to Ricki. FABULOUS, she writes in a bold

141

script. EVEN THE OLD FART SEEMS TO LIKE IT. Tyler has received a cable from his lawyer saying that the trees will be down within the week. and it appears that Fondue Reedy was not bonded. so Tyler is being sued for half a million dollars by Reedy's wife in Tennessee.

Tyler wonders about the trees—whether they will leave stumps upon which he can put at least some birdseed. and he short-dreams that one of the trees will fall on their house so he can collect insurance and move to a tree house. But then. after the first daiquiri. he realizes there is no escaping Dutch elm on the North American Continent. And he recalls reading of a new hybrid poplar which grows five to eight feet in a year. and calculates that he will be fifty-two before it would be even half the height. much less the width. of his lost elms.

It's hurricane season. that record year: the hotel holds only Tyler and Travis and a convention of roller-bearing salesmen. enormous men who apologize often for carrying on. who amaze the natives with touch football on the beach before cocktails. Fun-loving. homesick men who wolf their venison. wild turkey. tuna. artichokes. and enchiladas after smiting each other with heavy forearms. flinging a ball the shape of this ancestral island. and engagingly. shyly. ask Tyler's permission to dance with the only lady. Travis. She is fantastic. no doubt about it. The mariachi band with saxophone is all Mayan giggles as a dozen men take turns with Travis on the floor. their heavy sandy hands on her bare midriff. so polite they break your heart. She hardly has time to eat her dinner. and Tyler refuses to dance: he hates dancing, in fact, along with movies, cards, and night clubs. On leave from a particularly dramatic rumba, Travis asks Tyler why he's got his head in his hands. "Jealous?" she asks.

"I'm just sorry I don't give you what you want," he says. "And I can't imagine why you want it."

"You've always done everything for me but really love me, Tyler."

'Not a bad track record,' Tyler thinks to himself.

"I've never had a better time in my life," Travis says. "I could stay here forever."

Tyler withstands the obvious.

"What I hate most of all," he says, "is that we have begun to treat each other like everyone else."

Travis gives him a devastating but genuinely affecting smile. She has regained her youth somehow; the sand, the tan, her eyelids still pale from the sunglasses, glow like plankton from her thermal face. Her lips are frosty, and the nice Indian boy who brings their *chiles rellenos* can't keep from staring. It is now a question of which one of the diners is nuts. Travis has a sinking feeling, a suspicion, that it might not be she.

"You always put things in such a negative way," she begins. "What's wrong now?"

"It just seems, Travis, that you are getting smaller — smaller and smaller."

"I'm sorry, Tyler. I guess in a way I'm just a mess."

"A tiny mess, then."

"*You* are like an animal. I don't know what kind. Or rather a lot of different animals — a pack of bears, maybe, in one cage." Then she begins to weep softly, her turquoise pendant shivers in her cleavage. "maybe I've got sunstroke." she says.

"You were born with bloody sunstroke, Travis!"

A conventioneer wedged behind Tyler to the railing, and flung a tortilla into the floodlit lagoon. Orange blunt lipless mouths rose to scarify the surface. "Here's some Mexican meatloaf for ya, fishies."

Travis excuses herself, taking the napkin with her. Tyler moves to the bar among the chorusing, pummeling salesmen. It takes fifteen minutes to explain to the crestfallen waiter why they didn't finish dinner. "Hot," says Tyler, lying, sticking out and pointing to his stippled tongue, and the Indian performs the "this no Popsicle country" shrug.

Travis walked down to the beach in front of the other hotels, clenching her fists, regaining control in the soft night. At the end of the beach was a coral promontory and a cross gouged into the pocked rock. "A gallant diver," the inscription read, "*Jesus Jesus* was lost here." The path wandered off to a swamp. Travis turned around and walked back past the hotels where everyone was eating. Just before she entered the hotel, however, in a bar of moonlight between the stunted palms, she saw a couple, at least twenty-five years older than she and Tyler, holding hands, the woman kissing the man's shoulder as he kissed her forehead. Travis burst into tears and ran up to her room.

FRIDAY

Tyler lurched in an hour later after a medley of college favorites.

*I'll eat the veg-a-tables
you eat da meat.* etc.

Travis was lying face down on the bed. half naked. a water tumbler full of crushed cigarettes spiraling a blameless aureole of menthol about her body. The paleness where the bra strap was contrasted nicely with the dark racing stripe between her buttocks. "Don't slam the door." Travis said into the pillow. "please don't kick the chairs. Why do you get in these moods?"

Tyler lay down on his back with Travis and slipped off his shoes and socks. Then she undid his zipper but couldn't get the slacks over his numb hips. "I was never very good at this." she said softly.

It was the first time they had been in the same bed in four months. Tyler stared at the two pairs of feet. one up. ladylike. the other's arches hooked down over the edge of the bed: fish and fowl. Then he turned on his back to take his own pants off.

"There's a fly. Tyler. It's driving me batso."

Tyler got up and turned out the light. "When he goes to the light in the john we'll lock him in."

"I miss Sandy." said Travis. sobbing.

"Shit. I miss 823 and 824!"

"Tyler. isn't there any way we could make a living down here?"

"Do you realize. love. that my little toe is almost the same length as my big toe? That is rare…"

WHITE JAZZ

Travis's foot was beneath Tyler's thigh. 'The foot is indeed the noblest of beasts,' he thought, 'smarter than the stomach, more erotic than the brain.' Tyler grinned to himself, and began absentmindedly to knead Travis's delicate brown foot as he would squeeze the roe from a trout.

Gradually, effortlessly, Travis's toes assumed their own space, her feet parted from one another then flexed as they raked Tyler's thighs, her legs locked about Tyler's waist, whose toes were now definitely dancing, down and out.

In the morning, Tyler and Travis went out on their balcony in their lemon short-sleeved knee-length Caribbean pajamas. Beneath them in a clump of yucca and hibiscus a large lizard had already swallowed the legs of a tropical quail, but the bird was almost reflectively, it seemed, battering the lizard's skull to a pulp.

"I'm the bird," Travis said, "and you're the snakething, Tyler."

"Nope," Tyler smiled. "I'm the little birdie with the big bill."

"Look, they've stopped," Travis said.

"Let's get dressed," Tyler said, spanking Travis more than playfully. "I hear there's some great art down in the valley."

But the tale told by the machine of loving grace served only to make Sandy more imparient than ever. He has forgotten his vow, has gone one step too far; once again he is outside the calculus. He draws the console to him and types with one finger:

Then how to grieve?

There is an uncharacteristic pause of several minutes; Sandy's throat is waxen. There is some humorless judging going on somewhere.

```
ee:  5WL12
/s — /  —  — —
rw— —r—r—le.  5v12
you have mail?
```

Sandy retypes the command, and there is no caesura in the circuitry this time.

*Not to pass on the sadness please
This facility is closing down.*

A forlorn Sandman is dissolving. The pain is neither ironic nor localized, neither allegory nor allergy. He is beginning to sympathize with the General Anesthesia. "All we know for sure," Haas says, "is that the rate of increase is increasing." Sandy wishes to be interrupted, intertwined, enthralled. He desires total passivity, that things should just *stop* for just a moment; he repudiates his memory, insufficient as it is, he wishes to be beyond waiting; he desires only to be a good consumer, his indebtedness paid up right to the last compounded daily interest point, and exercise the array of options that are unique to the people of Heaven and what they call home. No one to command, no one to obey, no one to transgress... No aura, no sense, no information, no time, no context, No Thank You. THE TROUBLE IS NOT IN YOUR SET.

At home, on the ARTS Channel, there is much starting of cars. Also, a Spanish couple in a sleeping bag on the beach. The translated sub-titles stencil the bag and make a nice counterpart with the waves.

¿Tu mi mujer?
[Are you my woman?]
Muy poco, tan poco.
[So little, how very little.]
Adelante! Adelante!
¿Y todo?
[This also?]
Va deslizando subaba!
[What idyllic drool!]
No ha terminado.
[I haven't finished yet.]
No, no me jodas.
[Stop screwing me around.]
No habla mierda!
[Shut up, you shit!]

Now there is a pleasant woman carving a turkey. "*Y Enfin La Vida,*" she says so softly that it goes untranslated.

FRIDAY

At *El Cielito Lindo* the air is incipient fire, an air of unprecedented seriousness. *The Conquerors* are moody, and they phlegmatically stomp out the bitter white jazz.

> *The thing about the dead man blues*
> *Is that a dead man*
> *Don't have any blues*
> *So it's a kind of joke*
> *Those blues.*
> *Don'tchaknow. Don'tchaknow.*

The Sandman hides in the murmuring meadow of the bar, the weeds come to his chest, the undergrowth is damp and tangled; beneath the brittleness of a sea of seed pods. He will take it easy. He will be selective. He feels that he is on the threshold of something and, while knowing this feeling is an illusion, nevertheless savors it. Tonight he will be nobody else, not even himself. He will be like the pure dog in the alley with his scraps, his dork unsheathed like a red turnip.

> *The gods are all humbled*
> *Sit and weep, yeah sit and weep*
> *Their lips drawn tight*
> *They crowd like flies*
> *Around the sacrificer*

Sandy is aware of a dark head on his chest, and brown arms

about his waist. He cannot see her face. She is rocking on the balls of her feet as if drunk. She whispers in his ear.

"You could have any woman you want, I know. You'll be good to me, I know."

There is only one storification, one tale worth repeating. It goes like this: A girl is asleep. You wake her up. You give her something to eat. You send everyone else away.

But Sandy is not the happy dog with the maroon schlong. He is inattentive, abstracted. Another winsome lissome loser, he is thinking, but as it turns out he has made a serious mistake and back at *The Left Bank* he asks her, staring fixedly into her blooming labia, how it was.

"All right," she said.

"Just all right?"

"All right is just that. Listen to the word. *Alllllllll* right!"

Sandy looks, listens.

"How come you're looking at me like that, hey? Hey, stop that. You make me nervous."

The Sandman rolls over and throws his left arm over his left eye. He has the distinct feeling they are being watched. Slowly, like a gun turret swinging out to sea, his right eyeball rolls westward in its socket. The tear ducts are swollen but the valves hold. He swallows his gasp. He has never been so astonished. For Tyler and Travis are sitting at his coffee table, each a little diaphanous perhaps, but palpable enough for all that. They have completed the word. They are out of the game.

Tyler is sitting cross-legged in his weekend clothes: khaki slacks, combed cotton shirt, and boating shoes. Travis is dressed to the teeth, the yellow angora suit for traveling, nylons and walking shoes, exposing her best features, those trim ankles which never left her, and which were the last thing he saw of her. He remembers the doctors better than the patient. The agonized Filipino internist, the Dutch anesthesiologist wringing his hands. Tyler is absently drumming his fingers on the table staring around the cornice of the room; Travis is fingering the rubberized curtain, taking stock. They seem pleased enough or at least uncritical. The room is neat! Sandy whews and then cries out.

"Well, was I gentle enough? Did I last long enough?"

"Wow," she says, "are you ever insecure. This is terrible."

"I wasn't talking...to you. I'm sorry."

"Then you're crazy, 'cause I can tell you're not a cruel person."

'So sweet and sensical she is,' the Sandman thinks. He turns his back on Travis and Tyler.

"You're holding me too tight," she says. "Don't worry, I'm not going to leave."

Sandy screams at Tyler and Travis. "Get out! Leave me alone."

"I know you don't mean that. You're being irrational again."

"Don't pay any attention to me," Sandy gasps. "I don't know what's happening to me."

"I'm scared too. Want to talk about it?"

'Oh this *talking* business,' Sandy thinks.

He gazes at Tyler and Travis. They were chatting now, but

he can't hear what they have to say. They are covering their mouths with their hands.

"What," he yells, "what?"

The girl is now the one who is abstracted and bemused. "Does your craziness scare you? You know many people who are crazy?"

But the Sandman's thoughts are only of Tyler and Travis.

"I used to think *I* was crazy," she went on. "All I could think about was how fast I would lose everything. First the crow's feet, then the behind goes, the breasts removed, the pituitary, cysts on the ovaries, a lot of cancer in my family I'll tell you; anyway what I was scared of, it turned out, was not craziness, what worried me was benignity, if that's a word...please don't hold me so tight. I can't get my breath...there, that's better. Don't look so forlorn. You change your face so much. You looked like a little child. Then like a king for a while. But now you look so sad. Come on, I'm the only one who's got anything to lose. You have all the advantages. Offhand, I'd say you need me. You might get tired of me, of course, but I won't bother you. How do we work things? I mean, give me a plan."

Tyler and Travis have begun to play hearts.

"Get out, go away," Sandy moaned.

"Look, I will if you really want me to, but not until you stand up straight, look me in the eye cold sober, and tell me to get the hell out."

Sandy could barely breathe. The pain extended like a meathook from his sinuses to his lungs. He couldn't help himself. He screamed and raged at Tyler and Travis.

FRIDAY

"O.K. But you've really got something, you know. There're a lot of slugs out there, believe me. There's a couple of things you should know, though. First, I'm somebody special, you'll see. Second, it's better for you if you're devoted. You'll see."

Tyler had stopped in the midst of a deal. Travis had an index finger against her lips. They were listening carefully to what he would do.

"The third thing to remember is the hardest," she went on. "And that's this: Sometimes you only get one chance. So I'll be going now."

Sandy nodded almost with relief. He was stunned.

"Look," she said, tying her shoes. "I don't care how strong you are. Look at you lying there like a board! You wouldn't know what to do with help if you got it. But me, I need support. And freely given too. You think you could get it up for that? I don't care if you're depressed even. Just treat me right, hear? That's my theory."

She dressed inconceivably fast, smiling at him. She was not striking — her ears stuck out, she was pigeon-toed, a little knock-kneed — but her smile and bright eyes gave him a profound ache. She said her name was Winnie Tranquilla. Italian Episcopalian apparently. Her neck was so fragile, she bore her head with a perpetual sense of surprise, a dignity beyond all reason.

But this was nothing compared to his astonishment when Tyler and Travis threw down their cards, sprang to their feet, and, without so much as a wave or a nod, followed Winnie out of the room with unconcealed disappointment.

The arm falls again over the left eye. Haas will not believe this. Some age-old assumptions are going to have to be put on the line.

"Well, it's come to this, Haas. I guess I got to show my love, shew my love now, Haas. Haas? How do you *show* your love? Haas? Haas?!"

A love without subtitles. This is the hardest thing.

Saturday

It is nevertheless possible to assemble
from highly unreliable individual components
a system with a high degree of purposiveness.
by a lavish provision of redundancy...

REGURGITATION DAY. The meat for which the week's grass is given. Main Events were the *Zoo Fair* and the *Game of the Week*, "for those who want to stick around the house," or so suggested one Ron Flaherty, who claimed he was the new vice-president for corporate affairs for Channel 27–407. He signed off, instructing all to have a good weekend with the new station's license and motto: "There's nothin' I'd rather do/than happy talk on the Ray-Dee-O."

Although Sandy would have preferred the *Zoo Fair*, it was, after all, Art Entelechy's final game. While he had taken them to the play-offs twelve out of thirteen years, the Big Enchilada had always eluded the Rough Grouse. Perennial bridesmaids was the charge. Good, even very good; but they were always yet to gain the Kingdom.

There was no way to get to the zoo and back in time for the game. He would have to endure all Saturday morning until game time. It would be his greatest challenge in a great while. The Sandman was considering going for the swamp.

That morning at dawn, nine of Maintenance Man's colleagues, featuring a poochy Teamsterette flown in from the Regional Office, paid their final respects with a special procession. Cued by the CB, nine enormous orange tractor-trailers left the overpass where the rig had jackknifed, negotiated the cloverleaf, and moved at 15 mph out to the Church of an Epiphany, where as each passed, a crushed cap went over the heart. To symbolize the departed trucker, the second cab pulled no trailer, but a WIDE LOAD of pure air.

Sandy's projects were going badly. He was hopelessly behind on the *Human Resources* catalogue, as he had run out of categories. He had been forced to use a final four by Haas, who had scavenged them from another program — cochleous, scolecoid, sigmoid, and sinuvivulose. The *Post-Modern Gourmet Guide* was stalled, as he could not come up with a code to differentiate, much less evaluate them; "I know you all are trying hard, but the gazpacho needs a garnish, the galantine of duck was short on pistachio, the braised celery was soggy, the peaches Indienne canned, and the Ravigote Skri Lanka wasn't one..."; the *Bravery Index* was still in a hopelessly theoretical and unrealized state; "So many different kinds of courage!" he complained to Haas who nodded, it should be noted, without his usual smirk. He had exhausted his data in the Tyler & Travis file, and he could not come up with an execution algorithm for his own personal concordance. As for his girl Friday, Winnie

SATURDAY

Tranquilla, he did not believe her. It was only natural that everything would be repeated, that nothing is completed. The Sandman was losing his concentration. He had clipped his brittle nails to the quick.

Moreover, *The Left Bank* was disintegrating at an exponential rate since Maintenance Man's untimely demise. Down in the foyer the last free services had been crossed off.

>   Yours For The Asking!
>   What Do You Need?

>   ~~Bicycle~~
>   ~~Bridge Table~~
>   ~~Extra Blanket~~
>   ~~Pillow~~
>   ~~First Aid~~
>   ~~Heating Pad~~
>   ~~Ice~~
>   ~~Iron~~
>   ~~Hair Dryer~~
>   ~~Typewriter~~
>   ~~Sewing Kit~~
>   ~~Spot Remover~~

Even the Daily Schedule had been abandoned, and with it, any semblance of discipline.

>   7 Wake up
>   8 Breakfast
>   9 Self Awareness Synthesis
>   10 Dependency Group
>   11 Movement Group
>   1 Journal
>   2 Family Dynamics

WHITE JAZZ

    3 Integration Group
    4 After-Care Group
    5 Chalk Talk
    6 Dinner
    7 Visitors "Ask the Doctor"
    8 Free Time
    9 *Cielito Lindo*

He started down to the wreckroom but discovered that the 10 Depression Danger Signals had been posted on the Coke machine.

1. A general feeling of hopelessness and despair that pervades all of one's life.
2. Inability to concentrate, making reading, writing, and conversation difficult.
3. Change in physical activities, such as eating, sleeping, and sexual activity. Frequently, there are physical complaints with no evidence of physical illness.
4. A loss of self-esteem which brings on continual questioning of one's worth.
5. Withdrawal from others, not because of desire to do so but from an immense fear of rejection by others, even though there may be no basis for fear.
6. Threats or attempts to commit suicide which is seen as a way out of a hostile environment.
7. Hypersensitivity to words and actions of others and general irritability.
8. Misdirected anger and difficulty in handling most feelings.
9. Guilt feelings, when a person assumes he is wrong or responsible for the unhappiness of others.
10. Extreme dependency on others, which brings on feelings of helplessness and then anger at the helplessness.

He returned to his room to take stock.

SATURDAY

MY DAILY MORAL INVENTORY

LIABILITIES — Watch For:		ASSETS — Strive For:
Self-Pity	X	Self-Forgetfulness
Self-Justification	X	Humility
Self-Importance	X	Modesty
Self-Condemnation	X	Self-Valuation
Dishonesty	X	Honesty
Impatience	X	Patience
Hate	X	Love
Resentment	X	Forgiveness
False Pride	X	Simplicity
Jealousy	X	Trust
Envy	X	Generosity
Laziness	X	Activity
Procrastination	X	Promptness
Insincerity	X	Straightforwardness
Negative Thinking	X	Positive Thinking
Vulgar, Immoral Thinking	X	Spiritual, Clean Thinking
Criticizing	X	Look for the Good!

Things didn't look good.

And to top things off, Haas had been after him again, the very last thing on Friday, apropos of nothing, reminding Sandy that within the year they would achieve total transparency in the system, the lubric simplification of all interfaces, so that programmers would no longer be concerned with knowing how the system worked to operate it; functioning without anyone having to understand one iota of the architecture. "Total transparency throughout the entire society," Haas smiled. "Transparency is transformation, and transformation is wealth."

"Why don't you ever open up, Haas?"

"All you have to learn, Sandy, is to be able to see through people without feeling superior to them. I'll tell you about myself one of these days."

Sandy tried not to be insulted. With the new breakthrough, he would be moved on to other projects, no doubt — the once partially but emphatically understood, gradually evaporating to a few patches and fixes of memory, his expertise leaving him just as Tyler and Travis had done, without a clue as to what had brought and kept them together.

But Haas had made one crucial miscalculation, due to the very symmetry of his mind. For as the hierarchies of the system increased, it became increasingly impossible to discover what Sandy had programmed, without the considerable risk of rendering the system inoperative. In fact, he had already forgotten so much of what he had done, that tiny portion of his willfulness would remain alive and unlabelable within the system, for which he would receive neither credit nor blame, and which could never be removed or even identified — except at the expense of the entire system. So it was that the Sandman had an inkling of Modern Revenge. The lost self, a bit of sugar in the gas tank. To the degree he had forgotten, he *was*.

Sensing that he had been overpersonalizing his remarks, Haas took a skinny finger and tapped lightly but repeatedly on the dark and muscular wrist of his favorite colleague.

"What we must be willing to entertain..."

SATURDAY

"Oh, Haas, not again..."

"Yes indeed, what we must be able to entertain, and this is not necessarily scary, is that because of the way we have lived very recently, the way we make do with what we've made, that a third area of existence — a kind of spiral nebulae — now exists between us and the world. It is clearly the adaptation of the brain to multistimuli, a mind-fetus aborted into the world, to save both fetus and host. Anatomically, perhaps the pancreas, the shock organ for the entire system, would be similar — except this is, well, *out there,* hanging in front of our very eyes! It is the final, hear this, destruction between subject and object — it is not a language, not a mathematics, and it is not, most emphatically, emotional. It cannot be plugged into. It is the Gross Fact of our time. It cannot be wielded, but like most lower forms of life, it rebels if you try to suppress it. The overwhelming temptation will be to name it. Only those strong enough to resist this, to carry it with some disinterest and dignity, like a child carries a balloon, will come to understand its properties...."

"Could this bugger give you headaches?"

"Yes, I suppose. But steady work too. But we won't speak of it again. I can see you are already searching for metaphors...."

Sandy's room was getting colder. He couldn't go to the control room; he could never enter the steam tunnel again. Somebody's children were hiding down there. Only a week ago, while searching for Maintenance Man, he had stumbled across a boy and girl, not more than seven, asleep in each other's arms on a pile of old drapes, their heads crowned with the remnants of box lunches. Their skin was mottled in the shadows, their dirty ovoid empty faces crosshatched and laced up tight; raised seams of indifference.

Back on his back. Left arm over left eye. The photos of Tyler and Travis are losing color and finish every day. And the film, the processing fluids seem to be enveloping Sandy; what was a vibrant virtuoso print is reverting to a sharply etched but somber negative. His parents' sky is now a hideous blue; the variegated autumn foliage now all of a piece, a garish sun-flare. The lake is purpling and there is the smell of fish everywhere.

He found himself on the expressway, the Pontiac weaving some, and ultimately in the only haven he could count on — the nearest of Dr. Onarga's mall offices. The girls in white were thrilled to see him; how did he know there were two no-shows? The wait will be respectful but tolerable. They give him coffee, bun, and the morning newspaper. Onarga's glistening head appears in the doorway and he waves, perfunctorily flip-flopping an X-ray. Sandy's sighing had all but subsided as the girls took him in and laid him down in Dr. Onarga's Mediterranean Room. His physician was in excellent spirits.

"Nice that you could stop in. The results of your atomic testing are definitive, and just as I thought. This test measures the lowest unit of energy, the encapsulated replica of your entire genetic program. You are in touch with all the higher laws — which accounts for your vague air of superiority, no doubt. But it's the lower laws that are the most difficult to comprehend. Calm the lower body, quicken the mind, eh? At any rate, your electron balance, the inertia-force ratio, is on the high side of normal. But the neutron level is down—you lack capacity for fusion, which is not a revelation to you, I don't suppose, and your protons—*well*, there's apparently no assimilation going on in that quickly aging system of yours at all...At this stage of your enfoldment the triune balance of your creature forces is completely out of whack. So *hoc habet!*—False Digestion! I eyeballed it, here's unequivocal proof. I suppose you want to know where we go from here?"

Sandy's eyes were rolling on their own, clutch disengaged.

"Your typical response to multistimuli is to fill the void with positive energy. And it's true you possess considerable molecular talents. But this is not an efficacious response to Bad Light. You cannot beam Bad Light back at itself. One begins with the gums; we invariably end with universal complaints."

"I got trouble with the terminology!"

"Rather! Do not confuse stimuli with clues. Blocks to knowledge are not removed by more knowledge. It is your very illness that centers you now. It is the illness that attracts energy. Too much of this energy is being crystallized in the system. Too quickly, it reconverts to mass..."

"I still don't understand what I'm supposed to concentrate *on*..."

"Hey! It's *not* a question of concentration! The body is mostly fluid. Real pliable, believe me. These fluids respond to the images they carry. These images become superimposed because they exist in time/space you cannot comprehend. They tend to cancel one another out, become equivalent. You inhabit many universes, all in existence simultaneously, which can be somewhat confusing. These universes are mostly light. The nearest universes are Bad Light. We don't care about this light's speed, how it bends, what all. The point is whether it's good or bad for you. Bad Light puts increased pressure on the glands. The ingestion of Bad Light sets up an artificial image in the system. This activates *False Digestion*. The system goes through the motions of digestion, but there's no nutrition. The information goes in all right, but it's not processed. You must be prepared to take a good hard look at yourself."

"What am I supposed to see?"

"Simple. You must recognize your powerlessness. You must exercise the power of submission. There are precedents."

"That's easy enough. It's enforced upon me every day of my life." Sandy was becoming uncharacteristically bitter.

"And every night? Be wholehearted now."

"Well...in a different way."

"Your problem resides simply in a vestigial defiant individualism. You must surrender!"

"O.K., O.K., I surrender. If it will ease the pain. But the terms? Are there not always terms?"

"Compliance is not surrender, Sandy. You can absorb no more Bad Light without irreversible damage. Tell me, are you willing to *ask* for help?"

"From you?"

"From whatever higher power you recognize. You cannot

live in a deprived state. Put your patience at the center of the unmanifest..."

"Hey, what kind of name is Onarga, anyway?"

"Easy there. This relationship will remain on a professional level. You're not the sort who will attract sympathy, you know."

"I'm a little scared, Doc. This is getting very deathy."

Onarga had turned his back on him. Sandy was aware of all his fluid levels.

"O.K. It's late in the game, Doc. I *need* help. There it is. I'm *asking* you. I put myself in your hands. Nice, huh?"

Onarga half turned with half a smile. His fleshy temples glowed with health. He spoke very softly.

"I cannot take on the burden of your problems. That would destroy the evolution of the therapy. You, not I, are responsible for your recovery."

"I don't see how I can be responsible *and* surrender."

"It's not an easy concept to grasp."

Sandy wished he were not lying down. He could not rule out the possibility that Onarga was a fraud. But he also had to be prepared to accept that a fraud could be right.

"Is it possible that what's happening is that I'm sending up, sort of, a balloon to...to ward off Bad Light?"

"You're intellectualizing again. Pop that balloon!"

"Pop it?"

"Pop it."

"Then there's nothing between me and Bad Light."

"If you surrender, the Bad Light will go right through you.

No resistance, no reflection. No reflection, good digestion."

Apparently the Doctor had activated a signal, for all four allergatrixes had appeared around him, little coils of concern in their smooth foreheads.

"Don't balk at the consequences"—Onarga's team nodded in unison at this. "No real decision can be made until *you're* convinced you've hit bottom."

Onarga turned to leave the room. "Of course, if you choose *not* to make such a decision, I'll nevertheless do what I can to prolong your life."

The left arm slipped off his eye as the girls raised the chairback.

"Well, you know," the Sandman said, "I like him better than I did."

How he endured to game time, no one would ever know. He horsed the Pontiac home against heavy traffic. And even then they tricked him with an hour of introductions, banners, interviews, reruns, and commercials; Entelechy would tell him later, privately, that his arm had stiffened during the festive prelude.

The first half was a hard-fought but cautious affair. The Rough Grouse's collapsing, stunting defense forced the Mad Dogs to settle for three field goals. Entelechy engineered two model time-consuming drives, mixing off-tackle slants from his two mediocre setbacks, with short flare passes to his slender wingback, who possessed neither spleen nor drive but remarkable balance. All other receivers were kept in to block, nearly doubling his set-up time, according to Sandy's stopwatch. On their second drive, the Rough Grouse had third and one on their own forty-five. Entelechy ran both backs into the line on a crossback, trotted with false dejection into the solitude of the backfield, faked a flare to the wingback who was smothered by a red-dogging linebacker, then turned 180° and hit his tight end who had come off a mime block; a wobbly spiral but twenty yards from the nearest defender. He scored at an amble, and threw the ball into the second deck.

The most remarkable thing, however, was that Entelechy had also faked out all three cameras completely, so that the play was forever beyond the frame; beyond rerun and history itself. If not the most spectacular ever, it was certainly the only play of Entelechy's career that would never be subject to interpretation. When the half ended, the Grouse seemed in thorough command as they moved off the field with their high arching, tub-thumping Grousewalk.

Sandy opened a beer and leaned back, closing his eyes, dozing during the first-half "Highlights" which fairly crackled with commentary on *The Lost Play*. The halftime show was punctuated by cutaways to the *Zoo Fair*, where there was a contest to costume wild animals, domestic animals, and reptiles to see which genus could be made most human; "Animals Are Beautiful People." In the reptile class, an abstracted anaconda, dressed up in wire-rimmed spectacles, porkpie hat, and a striped cravat eight feet long, took first place. Between the pregame warm-up and the postgame wrap-up there was no purview.

But when they introduced a new color commentator, one

WHITE JAZZ

Francine Bates-Entelechy, the Sandman started. She came on as a good-looking, strong-featured woman, with long ash-blond tinted hair.

"It's only fitting, Fran, that at the very moment your husband is ending his career, you're beginning your own — which we hope, of course, will be no less illustrious in its way."

"Yes," she pursed an odd little smile, which Sandy recognized as strangulated fury but which on the tube came across as cursory panache, "of course I don't intend to trade on my husband's name."

Gary, the co-anchorperson, pulled at his thin lapels and self-consciously checked the monitor. "Well, Fran, the Rough Grouse are up, 14 to 9, and it looks as though they may *fin*ally pull it off. Would you care to analyze the action so far, a kind of...insider's point of view, sort of?"

"Well, all I can say, Gary, without betraying old confidences, of course, is that the Grouse have followed their game plan to a tee, and if they stick with that, there's no way they can lose. Art can't throw long anymore, it's no secret. And the running game was always merely credible. So if they get behind, if Art has to play catch-up, go for the big one, you can forget it. The Grouse will go down again."

"We appreciate your frankliness — good to know where you're coming from, Fran — and we'll be looking for any deviation from the game plan, you betcha. I see the teams are back on the field, no injuries so far — of course, Art has never missed a game due to injury in his entire career. What do you attribute that remarkable stamina to, Fran?"

SATURDAY

"Well, Art has played hurt plenty. Maybe most people don't know that. I think the answer is that Art has a high pain threshold. Basically, Art's totally insensitive..."

"Remarkable, Fran, remarkable. Well, we've only got a minute to go...hey, what's it really like to share the life of a famous sportsman like Art there?"

The smile went sour, but only for an instant, as Fran's hands fluttered, then clenched. The voice was only slightly nasal.

"I put off my life for the children and my husband, and now it's time to start my own. I'm going to write all about my life with Art in a book."

"But what's he like *off* camera?"

"*Exactly* the same. Expressionless."

"We wish you well with your writing, Fran. There's always room for knowledgeable women in sports, but can't you give us, you know, in the thirty seconds we have left, say, just an idea say, to sum up sort of, the thrills and sorrows of thirteen long seasons in the league?"

"Sure. Monday night we go over Sunday's game films. Tuesday, the next opposing team's latest films; Wednesday night, the opponent's old films; Thursday night, Grouse versus opponent films; Friday night, selected slow-mo individuals, so Art can get into his rhythm; and Saturday, Art usually brings home some great-games-of-all-time films, you know for inspiration, like?"

Sandy saw then how Fran had lost her hero, too.

"Well, nobody," Gary broke in, "seems better acquainted

to help us with our play-by-play than Fran Bates-Entelechy. Fran, we've got the kickoff coming up right now."

Sandy was anxious. Was Art privy to this? Art was in fact on the screen now, with two cans of low caloric beer and two long-legged beaver ladies.

"Consistency is the name of the game in beer as well as ball," an omniscient voice related. Art's weak chin and broken nose nevertheless radiated a certain dignity as he stood blushing between the two girls, clutching the two-fisted beers like grenades.

The Rough Grouse received the kickoff, and Art had them moving inexorably once again. The game plan had not changed, except that now he often put his wide receivers into inverse banana patterns, to open up the middle for deft short passes under the coverage, whenever the drive stalled. Sandy calculated that Art had earned some $41,000 for his workmanlike performance in the first half. He wondered what would become of *him* when Art retired. For in the seasonless air, his life for thirteen years had been calibrated, punctuated by Entelechy's playing schedule. Entelechy's career exactly spanned the time frame of Sandy's sexual experience; in fact, Entelechy was the *only* continuity Sandy had ever experienced in American life. You forget the sex but not the sport.

"Oh Jesus, it's fucking Jell-O time."

This was Fran, who in her initiation had apparently forgotten to turn off her microphone.

Of course she was right, and, as Gary corroborated, this

SATURDAY

could well spell big trouble for the Grouse. The Grouse had never fared well on gelatin, their only loss of the year coming on it in the second game of the season. It destroyed the home advantage, it varnished the precision of their attack which was hardly tanklike. Entelechy could not set up on his bad knees properly in the stuff, and their light no-block lanky setback's quickness was negated. In the days before the gelatin era, Entelechy would simply change his cleats to appease the elements, and his completion percentage was a remarkable 55 percent on mud or snow. But on gelatin the Grouse were 3 and 19 over the decade.

Gelatin had been introduced by the League Office when the Rough Grouse had moved into their new indoor stadium, an enormous aluminum A-frame with no stands, where they could play for the cameras and announcers only, and the crowd could stay in their homes, paying a subscription for the season — an ingenious device which reduced overhead to a minimum and allowed the club to use computerized direct mail to hype its audience. But when subscription income unaccountably slumped, the reportedly pious ownership decided that the environment was overly technologized, and therefore Considered Acts of God would be reintroduced.

So it was that cowled ducts were placed at each yard stripe, and at random intervals, determined by a secret scrambled code, great quantities of foamy gelatin randomly oozed forth upon the artificial playing surface — simulating wondrous wrath — challenging the best-laid game plans, skewing the gambling odds, and sending superbly conditioned athletes into gyrations, pratfalls, and goofy stunts worthy of the most violent cartoons. And whenever this happened — it was indeed the most gelatinous season in recent memory — by a special arrangement with the networks, bulletins went out, announcing "Jell-O disaster!" increasing viewers as much as 50 percent. There was in fact a special clause in all advertising contracts that if one was lucky enough to have one's spot occur during a Jell-O disaster, there would be a surcharge of 50 percent additional, a bounty gladly paid.

The players slowed earnestly, having made fools of themselves on gelatin before. And it was a particularly heavy flow today, ankle deep in some places on the field, so that the rhythm was more slogging than slipping — not all that different from the *El Cielito Lindo* stomp

The Grouse's small backs fumbled twice, but even without these lapses, the superior bulk of the Mad Dogs would have in all likelihood prevailed under such conditions. Entelechy's receivers could not get free, and when they did they invariably dropped the dying quail which became wobblier as the half went on. "While his spirals were never of the picture-book variety," Gary murmured, "Entelechy had everything to be the greatest ever, except for his smallish hands. He couldn't get a good one-handed grip. If his fingers had only been a quarter inch longer," Gary said, "he could have been better than near great. But you can't clutter up fame with the near great."

Entelechy had never really captured the fans' imagination. They resented his blandness, his wealth, his outside interests, his lack of an identifiable style, as well as his decision to retire early,

SATURDAY

relatively unhurt, unconcerned, uncrowned, uncanny, and unwon.

Ultimately, the Mad Dogs took over a shanked punt on the Grouse's thirty-four. Their unremarkable but persevering quarterback, Pelgesac, afraid to risk a pass or even a hand-off, ran repeatedly and utterly predictably off tackle behind his two massive Oriental pulling guards, as well as both creeping setbacks, until finally he slithered into the end zone for their only touchdown of the game, and even that was disputed vehemently by the Grouse, as the goal line was obscured in an opalescent sheen.

With 38 seconds left, Entelechy did exactly as Fran had predicted: tried desperately to go long with third and eighteen, and flung two passes — the first of which dropped harmlessly out of bounds, and the second of which, while perfectly thrown, at mid-arc turned into a throwaway baby. The Mad Dog free safety, one Enos McKinley, who had broken more than his share of collar bones with the meanest forearm shiver in the league, raised his hands up in glory, received the bundled child, ran in small excited circles, and then fell to his knees joyfully, cradling the gift as a horde of desperate Grouse descended upon him.

The clock counted them out, 16 to 14, the extra point superfluous. Enos McKinley ran into the locker room, holding the toothless bundle above him for the crowd, while Art Entelechy took off his helmet and smashed it to the ground in a hapless fury, his enforced laconism finally broken. The Grouse were again subdued, a hairsbreadth from Dominion.

They sought him out for the postgame wrap-up, in the losers' locker room, this breach of decorum justified by the fact that his retirement represented the end of an era. Entelechy was hunched in front of his locker, in nothing but a towel and shower clogs, his upper body considerably bruised but otherwise remarkable, in fact aged beyond his years; Art had drooping pectorals like an old man, and a small pot like a baby. Gary was at his side, one arm around the loser, the other cloying the microphone.

"I guess the Jell-O was the main factor, eh, Art? Tough luck, good buddy."

"I don't make the Jell-O. I just play on it."

"I know you're taking this hard, Art, your last game and all."

"People can't be too hard on themselves."

"That's a fascinating perspective, Art. Your heart's always been in your throat since you were a rookie. You think there was a psychological letdown in the second half?"

"If you can't play for the Grouse organization, you can't play for anybody."

"No, I mean did something go through the mind of the team?"

"The *mind* of the *team*? That's real funny. Boy that's a good one. The *mind* of the *team*.... Well, I've had some good times too. Good times most people haven't had."

"We're gonna miss you around here, Art. Will you miss the game, you think?"

SATURDAY

"Puke stinks as much at home as it does in the locker room."

"...I see. Well, what are you going to do, you think, now that you've retired?"

"Do? How the hell do I know? All I've done since I was eight is toss a football and talk to Nerds like yourself."

"You could play several more years, Art, you've never had a serious injury. Is it that you want to go out on the top?"

"This ain't the top. It's just the end. I'll never watch another damn movie, excuse the French, I'll tell you that. If you'd'a lived in my water for a week, friend, you'd understand."

"But I think the audience deserves to know what your plans are, Art."

"Hmmmpf. You got the straw. I do the grasping, huh?"

"I don't catch your meaning, Art."

"Well, I'll be all right. I've got some creative urges I'd like to get rid of. Now I'll have the time."

"Do you have any regrets? Like not winning the championship ever?"

"Well, if it has to be, I'd rather play good myself and us lose, than me play bad and we win."

"You were always a tough interview, Art, one of the toughest..." Gary had clearly run out of questions, and he looked desperately to his director, rolling his eyes.

"Hey," Gary said, suddenly elated, "here's your wife! Wad'ya know. Maybe she can cheer you up."

Fran entered the frame tentatively, and Gary put his free arm around her, hugging both the Entelechys with considerable force.

Then Gary intoned: "This is probably a first of some kind, folks. Fran, why don't you do an 'up front and personal' on your husband here?"

Art was having some phlegm problems. Fran was earnestly trying to appear bighearted.

"Art, honey," she wavered, squinting at the hastily scrawled cue card, "could you set the scene for us in the fourth quarter...when the Mad Dogs scored on their...only sustained drive of the day?"

"To tell you the truth, I don't remember. Why don't you ask the Defense?"

"What were you thinking when they were...on the march? Do you think you overrelaxed?"

"I wasn't thinking anything...except maybe about my hamstrings."

"Were you surprised that Pelgesac ran the ball so much himself?"

"No. Pelgesac's a ninny."

"How do you feel?"

"I seem to be all right."

Fran Bates-Entelechy's voice was so soft you could barely hear it.

"Do you think the Grouse game plan was too... conservative?"

"I forget how conservative it was."

SATURDAY

"Did you feel you could beat them right up to the last moment?"

"I still believe we could beat them. It's the way I was brought up."

Fran was becoming visibly nervous.

"Don't you think you ought to be more responsive to the people who have followed you all these years and who are responsible for your family's life-style? I mean that's just good sportsmanship."

Gary broke in. "Art? How strong a contemporary statement are you willing to make?"

Entelechy raised himself up, took the microphone from Gary, and spoke for the first and last time in his life directly into a camera. There were tears in his eyes, Fran notwithstanding. His tone was measured and he was careful to enunciate properly.

"Being a good sport is one of the most outstanding qualities a person can possess. When a team has lost a game, many people think sportsmanship consists of just congratulating the other team...but there's more to it than that. Not everyone can be good in sports, but everyone can be a good spectator. When a person is watching the game, he shouldn't constantly talk to the players or ride them because when he does it causes the players to become nervous and they might commit an error. If the members of the team lose the game they are playing, they should congratulate their opponents with all their hearts as well as their mouths. But spectators should be good sports too, inside as well as out."

Art Entelechy turned and disappeared into the shower room's clouds of steam, like a Norse god returning to the heavens. Except that his parts were very small. For a moment, all sixty millions could see was condensation on their screen, a frame of fog, and all they could hear was the dignified peripatetic clippity-clop of Entelechy's clogs on the tiles.

Of Entelechy, all that can be finally said is that even the simplest of his movements was moving, and this was a strangely happy day for Sandy's hero who would reemerge soon from the other side of the steam to his new destiny. At thirty-three, Art's indifference was a marvelous tonic. He had all the earmarks. If he did not make the Big Play, then he had made the routine, bearable. He showed that recovery is better than redemption.

'I will never,' Art was thinking as he soaped his groin, 'never be *seen* again.'

Tonight, Sandy is a volcanologist on his way to investigate a tremor in Guadalupe....

Sunday

The Letter shows us what God and our Fathers did;
The Allegory shows us where our faith is hid;
The Moral meaning gives us rules of daily life;
The Anagoge shows us where we end our strife.

"THIS IS the Reverend Moberly Markle, Deceased, spirit mouthpiece of 127–04, in the name of the spirit, good morning. You are having, no doubt, a rather difficult morning, so we shall, out of sympathy, be brief. We shall not discuss matters of habit or appetite. All spiritual centers shall be closed today so that you might function normally in the physical. We have all things but two; pride and solace... Please hold... Let us then limit ourselves to the extirpation of cancers. Later, we will entertain questions concerning the nature of Bad Light. We request, then, that this channel be returned to consciousness revitalized. You must forgive yourself. On this note we close this attunement... We can no longer hold the body...."

The Secret Channel had thus awoken him. Day of rest and gracious purpose rendered, Sandy is lining up with strangers for *El Cielito Lindo*'s famous Heritage of Woe Brunch. The hungry throng is subdued with mutual inspection and smug approval.

Sandy is uncomfortable, unfathomable, holding his plate. Such cleverly devised intercalary days, so hallowed and boring, make him actively yearn for the impermeable work week. Maestro Luncheon weaves like a praying mantis behind the buffet, petting the ice sculptures: the mandatory swan, pineapple pig, sublime rooster crouched above the capers and screaming at an entire bologna on the spit, self-basting with cherry jam.

The lobby decor has been modified again. Gone are the Revolutionary colors, as well as the antlers and plaids, replaced with grayed pastels, mauve, aqua; what was calm, stolid, and attenuated is light, soft, fluttering, billowing — Canyon Coral, Almond Blossom, Shy Zephyr, Poudre Blue, and Lemon Whip.

It is also very shadowy; a birthing darkness. Through the sliding glass doors he can make out Wanda June cleaning the pool with a vacuum hose, a horrid ribbed tube in her little hands. All the bloody marys and creamed chipped beef you can eat. Sandy fantasizes an alternative *à la carte:* shirred eggs with kippers and bangers, corn muffins, wafflettes with raspberry syrup, hashed browns blackened at the edge, the grits with tomatoes, scallions, and cheese which are missing too.

Despite the buffet, they have not been able to clean up from Saturday night. The floors are still littered with ashes and broken glass, and the air is heavy with the unmistakable scent of semen, which rises as from a chain gang in a misty morning chow line.

Sandy takes two plates, they are all he has in the world, and is startled by the PA system:

SUNDAY

The management wishes to show its appreciation to its faithful customers. Please join us on the roof garden for free liquid refreshment and an announcement.

Sandy blinked as he emerged into the hard natural light; his corneas have red and green dots in addition to the blue. Out on the roof, tar and gravel acrunch underfoot, the enormous air-conditioning condensors are swathed with bunting, the cubes of new air have been gift wrapped. Plastic orange trees in tubs have been placed at strategic intervals along the virgin helipad. Inflated uncircumcised cherubim are dirigible everywhere, blowing and glowing in the brief breezes. Their wings and genitals are very small, their buttocks and lips are very large, distended slightly by sacred conversation. They are florid more than ruddy, begrinned with a dreamy cheerfulness, and one of the pack leaders, carrying a trident, trails a banner from his short waist: KEEP SMILING! THE BOSS LOVES IDIOTS.

The gravel has been raked in orientalic swirls, and adjacent to the wading pool, beneath a striped canopy, a bar has been set up under an enormous rubber rubber tree. *The Conquerors* were as relaxed in the sunshine as he had ever seen them, and Ruby looked... well, wonderful in real light. Sandy knows; we're alone up here where there's no we're.

Ruby's warming up.

> *Oh, I put my right hand in.*
> *I take my right hand out.*

> *I give my hand a shake, shake, shake*
> *And turn you inside out,*
> *Oh...*

"I don't get this God is dead business," Wanda June said, suddenly at Sandy's side. "I mean people don't seem to miss God at all."

"I wonder what God did when he did nothing?" Sandy murmurs. "Anyway, how you feelin'?"

"I got my troubles, Sandman, there's something going around. But days like this I just don't care. You think that's dopey?"

The Sandman shakes his head sadly and by this Wanda June surmises that he would prefer not to entertain the question. He is staring down a vista, where at the end of a row of columns, he makes out an old man raking grass clippings in front of *The Golden Age*. His boundless rage, his unaccountable fury, has not abated. Wanda June drifts away.

Sandy downed his brunch leaning against the parapet of the roof garden. Everyone was here, it seemed. Dr. Onarga, sporting a rhinestone beeper in the hip pocket, dancing over there with one of the paraperiodontists. He realized that people like Onarga made their living from people who were intimidated by people like Haas. Art Entelechy was without popsy, de-Moiraed, but still mortified, swollen limbs protruding from his Bermuda shorts and alligator shirt. Entelechy was filling up with fluid, becoming a caricature of himself even as Sandy watched. Retired Grouse stuffed with human hematoma. So much for our belief in

SUNDAY

the superiority of the unpremeditated reflex. Everything can be explained by Careerism and Boredom.

Even Corrinne L. Huff had flown in from Akron for the event; she was talking with Paavo Nurmi's great grandniece and the pink woman now without guitar. All his ghostly babes together. And they sure as hell weren't talking about *him*. Somebody had taken away all his hip pockets. No place to put your wallet anymore. Hardly enough room for your scrotum, much less your money. Why do people fear dying alone and unloved? What difference does it make? Then? He recalled one of Haas's *rhapsodes*.

"Most systems absorb stress until they snap. The machines simply turn stress into more information. They don't snap. They don't overload. They simply become unequal to the task. We're approaching a moment rare and rapid. Some of us will flip into a new configuration."

So everybody was here, everyone except Maintenance Man, of course, and Winnie Tranquilla. Sandy ached for her. He missed her, it's the truth. Her spunk without spleen. Her energy without static. But he was strangely proud of her for not showing. Maybe she was putting him on about that one chance business? Was not everything to be repeated? Heartbreak was so generalized, why bother experiencing an individual instance of it?

In his confusion and pain, hung over and up, a credible person only to himself, the Sandman wanders the long roof of The Breakers. Above him, a biplane is barrel-rolling a message in white smoke.

JUDGMENT PREDICTED
MERCY PLANNED

Dr. Onarga, still dancing on his toes, waves to him without missing a beat as he twirls in the sunlight, his platinum digital watch like a laser.

"Hey, Sandy, you shall surely not die! I can probably cure you, but you got to *want* to be cured." He spins twice more. "You got to be *ready*, hear?" And then he spirals away, hands high above his head, snappy fingers all Sephardic Flamenco, his feet all Petipa. The Sandman turns with something like anger and nearly knocks a drink from the hand of Corrinne L. Huff, who is absorbed with the effortless hauter of the Caribbean maid in a pinafore, moving like Nefertiti among them with a tray of elastic canapés.

"Sorry," he blurts, "truly."

"So it's you, my man," she sizes him up scornfully. "You know it's over for people like you. You're going to be punished. Terribly punished."

"Just so long as it's not only me."

And with that she throws her Dubonnet in his face.

"Happy motoring, you asshole," she says softly.

"Hey, don't kid a kidder."

Wanda June is beside him again with a napkin. "I'm down, Sheba, down," the Sandman moans. She wipes his eyes and neck.

"Are you *ready*, Sandy?" Dr. Onarga pirouettes by him.

SUNDAY

"Wanda, you're a pal." The Sandman reconstitutes himself. "You are a true resource, a credit." He looks into her perfect eyes, reaches round and cups a small breast. "Maybe I'll kill that fucker," he murmurs absently.

"I could fall for you, Sandman. Always had a crush on you. But what you'd do with a Skank like me, I don't know."

"I'm off my feed, Wanda June...is there something I could do for you?"

"Ah, Sandman. Let's just take it easy today."

The Sandman was relieved. He will learn to be more dignified, more genuinely austere. A perfect gentleman.

"Lookit," said Wanda June, unbuttoning her vest. She has on a new lettered T-shirt.

CLARITY OF THOUGHT
CONSISTENCY OF ACTION
INTEGRITY OF THE WORD

"It's a new club," she smiled. Her perfect nipples distort the o's in Consistency and Action, like wandering electrons.

The pain was such that the only thing Art Entelechy knew to do was run, and after four circuits around *El Cielito Lindo* like a loose cannon, pulse at 175, the toxins going where they apparently just don't want to, his lungs finally opened up, and his boredom became authentic. The small footfalls took his measure — can't hold money/want loved ones back/want to get rid/of this strange illness/not much out there/after all/wasted my youth/on youth. It is only through short cruel and taxing sprints, his wise coach had said, that you can exchange plateaus. Amazing oxygen!

Then as Art settled into his second wind, he was aware of footsteps behind him, a faster more determined pace than his, coming right up on him. His reflex was to accelerate, not to be passed. But there was no sodium left in the hamstrings, his glottis closed like a day lily, and as he veered to give way, a fine-looking woman, hair one thick flying braid, drew even with him; "Track!" she bellowed. Art loved to see a lady sweat.

They ran at a speed where they could talk comfortably, as the good book says. Didn't quit for an hour. Watched in disbelief from the roof garden. On one circuit, a plate of macaroni fell right in front of them. And dead balloons everywhere. Breathless, flushed, their extremities throbbing, they reappear at the subfusc buffet in ragingly good spirits.

"Um, seconds," Art murmured, one arm about Corrinne, the other miraculously balancing two warm plates.

"You're an attractive, erotic, and altogether pleasant man, Art, but I don't think I could ever love you."

"Tell you right now, Cory, I want to be taken care of. I'm not shy about that."

"Art? How would you like it if the rules got changed in the middle of one of *your* games? It's not easy."

Art put down the plates and pondered that.

"Looks to me, Jocko, that you just like women, period."

Art was wondering who destroyed the spinach salad.

"I mean," Corrinne snorted, "I could be *any*body. Right?"

SUNDAY

Art sighed a bit, like he had been sacked. "Hey," he said softly, "everybody's mostly anybody." Corrinne pulled away from him.

"Go hire a nursemaid. Go back to your family."

Art put some Cool Whip on his Jell-O.

"Irretrievable. Forward fumble. Unforced error."

"But you just told me out there that *I* should go back. That's always the way, isn't it!"

"I think we should sit down," Art said. "That was quite a run."

Corrinne went to a banquette with her plate. Her fruit salad was running into her scalloped potatoes. She really did not like the *idea* of plates at all.

"What's the other ring?" Art asked. "The bad opal?"

"Oh. That's not to discuss on a first date. Well, it's like this. When I decided to lose my virginity, I told this older friend. He said think about it. I did and I asked him again. He said okay. He was wonderful. The next day he flew his plane over my parents' home. He even barrel-rolled. He was a pilot. Then the ring came with some flowers. I was lucky. I wasn't traumatized like my friends. I haven't been treated so well before or since."

"That's quite a story, Cory." Her thumbs were white about the plate.

"Actually, my son gave it to me. I think he lifted it. I like that in a man."

Art nodded, at what he didn't know. But he wanted genuinely to affirm her. Even her confusion.

"What I found, I guess," he began, "was that there isn't

much out there. I thought when I got freed up, I would have wonderful adventures. Then I thought because I was getting old, that I wasn't. Now I see that there ain't many adventures going on just now. No wonder people love sports so much."

Corrinne manufactured what used to be called a gaze, and it was no less pretty for all that.

"Artie, what *I've* realized is this. That all that shit they lay on you in Sunday school is true, in a way."

Art was hunkering over his food. "You know that one about 'pride goeth before a fall'? Well I always thought it meant that when you lose your pride, you fell. It's more complicated than that, isn't it?"

"Well, Artie, there's another thing you've probably overlooked. It's that we're in the only time of life that you can *really* change yourself."

Art leaned back and folded his arms. "I don't know why I like to eat so much. I think it has to do with not being fed."

"Maybe, Art, we should stop this courting. Maybe we could really take care of each other. Maybe we should just... proceed."

"Means dumping on even more people. Redumping in fact. Sometimes I wish I was harmless."

Corrinne frowned. "If we have to hurt them, let's hurt them together, then."

Art was on his third plateau. His brig was using Corrinne's wind.

"You know what I'll miss most?" Corrinne mused, not expecting an answer, "Eating alone. Now *that* was a treat."

SUNDAY

"Let's get changed," Art said.

Sandy and Wanda toured the rooftop's entourage arm in arm. The crowd was crushed, enfolded about the bar like iris fastening a June pond. And *The Conquerors* were picking up their beat with a swing version of one of their earliest arrangements, *Assassination Raga:*

> *You can get it all, if you give yourself up.*
> *Put yourself at the center, at the very most center.*
> *You can get anybody if you give yourself up.*
> *But you got to be willing, oh, you got to be willing...*

Wanda June has been challenged to a game of Ping-Pong, her only addiction, and Sandy is on his own again. But there, by God, standing in the door, there is Haas, disdainfully regarding the festivities, and is that *Mrs.* Haas with him, perchance?

"Hey, Haas, you finally made it, hey!" Sandy hugs Haas until he wheezes. But there is something eerie, something strange. Mrs. Haas is shy and dowdy to the point of...transparency. Sandy can see straight through Mrs. Haas. There is nothing the eye can fix on there, no bones or organs; Haas chooses not to introduce her, and she seems perfectly content with that. She is the tree in the forest that has not fallen because no one is watching it.

"I'm down, Haas, down, I'm a drag on the race. Let's hang one on, Haas, let's really get *out* of it."

Haas seems a little agitated in the crowd. Sandy offers to introduce him around but Haas demurs.

"Nothing," he says softly, arms asweep, "nothing but the richest possible inner life could justify all this. A culture which romanticizes truck drivers, for God's sake!"

Even when Sandy finally recorrals Wanda June, Haas shakes her hand limply and stares over her head. "Meet my terrific boss, Haas, hey, Wanda June." And when Haas turns obliquely, she rolls her perfect eyes and shakes a limp wrist mimicking detumescence. "See ya round," and she's gone again. It's a fact that Haas brings out cruelty in others.

"Haas, listen," Sandy's voice was urgent, "there's something I gotta ask you." Haas relaxed visibly as always when advice was asked of him.

"Haas, in a perfectable system is it true that you sometimes only get *one chance?*"

Haas screwed up his forehead.

"The general trend in a perfectable system is variety replacing intensity. But it's still possible, theoretically, that you could get only one chance."

"And, Haas, there's another thing been on my mind. I mean, it's easy enough to predict what's going to happen — but how do you go ahead and choose, knowing what the probability is, in spite of the odds, anyway?"

Haas smiled his baby smile. His papulae, his blebs, glowed.

"The system is in equilibrium, Sandman. There are no leaks. Error conditions and corrects error. Error conditions the correct path. You are raising the question, you see, of courage... This is

SUNDAY

a subject matter in which contemporary thought is not so strong...."

"Haas! This place is going to hell! None of my projects seem to be working out. I think I'm going through some kind of crisis, Haas. What do you think, Haas? You must have had a crisis once."

Haas's eyes widened and lightened. His acne seemed to darken with a hormonal firestorm. It would seem that whatever banal virus Haas has genetically is reappearing in the throng as an acquired characteristic. There are small pustules on all the lips and temples, masked with desultory swipes of ointments and gels. Sores, however, are rarely metaphors. There must be more to life than expelling death. Then Haas spoke, with the air of the man who knows he will have the last word.

"You're programmed to think of yourself in flux. You're putting the question badly. It is not that you have no freedom. It is just that it is not discernible at the general level of analysis. The relations are not entirely formal, but that does not mean they're a mystery. Informal relations, Sandman. They are quite sufficient."

Sandy was moaning. "Oh my country, my poor fucking country."

"Hey," Haas interrupted. "Now there's something you don't hear every day. Concern for the fate of this...this interracial conglomerate...? But let us consider reality for a moment. You blame change for your confusion. You believe that sloppiness is the price we have to pay for constantly adapting to new conditions. But *this*," Haas waved again to the roof garden, "this is not ephemeral. This will not go away. This cannot be changed!"

Haas went over and slapped a wall.

"This is con*crete,* reinforced with steel. Its stress points are precisely calibrated even before it's erected. This is anodized aluminum and polyurethane secured by a bed of indestructible fire-retardant styrene. It is not obsolete. It's concrete! This building will last for thousands of years! For your children, your children's children, as long as the roof is kept on it. It will exist for them whether you procreate or not. What you must decide is whether you want to be part of the circuitry, or not…"

Haas waved his hand in disgust at the throng's thralldom.

"You refuse to believe that society operates by a few inexorable laws which any primitive observer could grasp in a few moments. You seem incapable of understanding or accepting that when you moan about your bloody options. The Jell-O fate, which apparently causes much concern in these parts, is simply a procedure explicitly calculated to *appear* uncalculated…To make an egg, my associate, my colleague, it is necessary to subject a great many hapless omelets to unthinkable pressure!"

Sandy broke in, totally frustrated. "You're not going to get me to *rebel,* Haas. That's old hat for Christ's sake!"

But Haas was positively, inspirationally pissed.

"At age twenty-six — less than a year, Sandman — the bones in your back will join, and you will have produced your last living cells. This," he slapped the wall again, "is *not* obsolete. This is *concrete*. It is not a dream, it is *not* dreck, *not* trash. It is *not* ironic. It is aluminum, urea, titanium, magnesium, nitrate, brick, and bitumin! It will outlast Roman villas, the great châteaus and cathedrals, barring bombardment. Of course, it *looks* shabby and cheap. But so does Orvieto. But it is here to stay, my friend. This long and cogent road, no matter what eventually traverses it, will be always occupied by people very much like yourself, and someone, some small mutation like myself, will always turn up — behind schedule, no doubt, and at very high wages, insupportable wages — to service your useless rebellions with an acquiescent smile. Things may be running down, as you say, but nothing here is running down as fast as you are. In any event, all we can do now is make the general decline as slow and gradual as possible, and hope no one notices..."

Sandy did his best to appear unfazed. He had glanced once more at Mrs. Haas, and thought he could make out a shadow within her, a deflated football-like thing, suspended in her rib cage.

"Then there's just one more thing, Haas. Does it really matter...who you're...*with?*"

Haas suddenly went rigid and inarticulate. His scars were no longer illumined. He looked around suspiciously, glanced at his wife who was preoccupied with a flotilla of cherubim, and then, closing his eyes, grasping her fading hand, he gave a single, short but clearly affirmative nod.

"It was nice to meet you, Mrs. Haas." Sandy excused himself peremptorily. She was barely palpable in the harsh light. As Haas says, informal relations are quite sufficient.

"I don't like that man at all," Wanda June sneered.
"Well, *liking* him is not the point."

Professor Bob Jordan wove toward them, the blood vessels in his nose so dilated that his face seemed actually efflorescent. Sandy avoided Professor Bob as he did not want to discuss the Humanities, specifically the next week's assignment of *Huck Finn,* a thoroughly unbelievable story about a boy who runs away from his father and as a result experiences many difficulties and deprivations, only to find out at the end that his father was dead in the first place and that the trip was unnecessary.

The dancing was getting wilder, *The Conquerors* shifting into a viscous four-quarter beat.

> *There are many*
> *different gods*
> *but only one kind of man.*
> *If it is so pleasing, pleasing*
> *to behold,*
> *then why do you keep saying so,*
> *keep talking about it,*
> *keep pointing to it like that?*

Over Wanda June's shoulder he noticed that an anonymous couple had arrived. They were nearly magisterial in their entrance, come straight from the great world, arm in arm, apparently absolutely devoted to one another, yet quite aware of the effect their presence had upon the flaying throng. They seated themselves upon bar stools — the crowd, for the first time in Sandy's memory, actually made way for them — they ordered cordials, toasting each other with supreme consideration, arms intertwined. They were both of that tall well-formed person one

SUNDAY

almost prefers to see in middle age than youth: if they have lost something of their first bloom, they now excite not only affection, but a decided feeling of trust and confidence. Their easy manner of dealing with life's circumstances, their cheerfulness, their apparent unaffectedness communicated themselves right away, and their whole deportment was characterized by a noble decorum untouched by any sense of constraint. They seemed inseparable; insuperable.

Wanda June had spied them too. "They must be cops, plainclothes," she whispered.

Sandy did not answer. Had he chosen to, he would have called attention to the fact that they had far too much authority for gumshoe affiliation. He was staring again, eyes swimming with an unfamiliar litmus, puzzled by a convoy of trucks led by police cars advancing at cortege speed along the expressway.

He experienced a considerable wave of emotion as he took in the downcast competition in his peripheral vision. Such human resources gathered here, such unprecedented expertise and affective sensuality under the heavens' own roof vault! Why was it that they got so little for their efforts? How does one *gain* courage, Dr. Haas? How does one *surrender*, Dr. Onarga? Ball my fists, throw up my hands? Who holds your horse? Do you get to keep your side arms? How do you alter the steady state? Oh touch me, Mother. Pray for me, Father. It's not your fault that things didn't turn out! *His interests are wide ranging; his only guidelines; taste and quality...*

The couple had left the bar and walked hand in hand to the

center of the roof garden. It was not until the gentleman had whispered in the ear of the largest *Conqueror*, that Sandy realized it was Art, considerably straightened up and groomed out. Nothing in his experience prepared him for what was to follow.

Corrinne moved out smartly, twirled and extended her own throwing arm. Entelechy met her on his toes, and before you knew it they were doing the horrific, no holds barred, Dance of the Adults; *The Cost of Doing Business.* You describe the property, you exercise the option to buy, and the balance is due at closing. The prudent buyer will pay no more than he would for an equally desirable property. Yet the rule of prudence does not always apply.

There is no sending or receiving between these two, no axioms, no results, no electricity, no magnetism; they had been placed here by powers and events beyond them, they were dancing not a style but contiguous histories, defined by the circumstantial air as much as the simple math of the central nervous system, a slow magnanimous improvisational twirling, capsules and fluids, the capsules stacked neatly, but within them the fluids seek their own level. Against unspoken resistances, adventitious obstacles, they have ceased struggling, and to Sandy's surprise, this does not look at all like death. So that's the steady state!

They circled slowly about the floor, caressing every curvilinear inch of space. Corrinne is no longer a mean man, and Art no longer old womanish, put a pure long lever in the sparkling light. Art held her hand high above them as she twirled, climbing the wall of worry, and she swooned backward into his arms as the

SUNDAY

music finished. The whole roof broke into applause as they relinquished the floor.

And then Sandy broke his vow never to speak of Entelechy's profession in his presence. "Hey, Art? What you gonna do *now?*"

Art rolled his eyes. Corrinne looked downcast. Sandy saw Art's jaw muscles bunching; the era of his jowls was underway. Entelechy's new life awaited them all: a buffet of unknown covered casseroles, stretching away to infinity.

"Trouble with sports," Art said, "is that it's too serious. I'd like to get into *total* entertainment."

Corrinne nodded affirmatively.

"Endorsements," Art muttered, "voter registration. New rare diseases, things like that. But with a *script*. No more interviews...And no more visits to crippled children!"

"I thought you handled Fran, Art, as well as could be expected," Sandy said.

Entelechy was kneading his right forearm.

"You knew she got fired, I guess."

"What? No."

"She blew it. They canceled her contract. Said she was too difficult off camera. She blamed me, of course. Said I was uncooperative. Well, shit. I was counting on getting some of that alimony back. They sure pay pretty good dough, those TV people."

The pinafored Caribbean maid passed by them with a tray of water chestnuts wrapped in bacon. She was losing her good humor. Her eyes and nipples were hard as obsidian.

Corrinne broke in with her mouth full. "We have our *whole lives* ahead of us now," she said emphatically. Sometimes the prospect of new happiness will make us say things that sound trite.

Art was rambling on.

"First I'm gonna get my knees rebuilt. Then I got an offer from one of those schools where you teach what can't be taught, ya know.... Football's the springboard to life."

The crowd was becoming agitated, and Sandy slipped away before Art had a chance to finish. He couldn't believe that Entelechy was going to have to live more or less like Sandy, that from this day on they would be...indistinguishable. Would Entelechy now be interested in frames of Sandy's life? Was it now up to Sandy to entertain *him?* That might be a good idea for everybody, to exchange films of their own risk-adjusted lives; rather than meeting so often so desperately, so *publicly* — the exchange of game films would lend a certain spirit of mutual deliberation, a necessary detachment, even confer a certain dignity and celerity to the proceedings. Entertainment and criticism all of a piece; everyone their own star, looking for the repetition in the replays, the precision of the slo-mo, the successful pattern that becomes, by definition, the weakness to be exploited....

A fine sporiferous plan was aborning in the Sandman's mind, nothing short of a community rescue effort. They would open an eating casino where people could nourish themselves in enforced decorum while waiting out those long painful interstices before *El Cielito Lindo* opened — no longer reduced to a captive prowling of the expressways or other serial hiatuses.... They would use Art Entelechy's name, *Artie E's Nice Nihilism,* and he would preside as host, his glad post-passing arm thickening with good cheer as he wove giggling but graceful amongst the tiny tables. Wanda June would cohost, or real-host actually, as she would head up service; her loyalty and great good-heartedness finally having a palpable object, a true clientele. Sandman would program the marketing, accounting, and inventory with a thoroughness and effortless precision that would free them all. The chef would be no problem and the least significant part of the operation — his main qualification would be his capacity for genuine self-effacement.

In place of the menu, each guest would first receive a printout of the most recent *Post-Mortem Gourmet,* which would rank their competition in descending and exponentially invidious order, passing on to their guests a truly certifiable wisdom with no expectations. You may take this home with you, a better bone than any chop.

This is to be followed by the mandatory parody dish of their rivals — *real* laughing turtle for example, a land terrapin fattened on mussels and seared live on his belly, *table d'hôte*. This shall be neither despised nor eaten, as every night there will be a guest chef, Pauline say, or Bruno, the Wharf Rat even, all the animals who are beautiful people, invited to prepare their specialty at tableside upon a tiny wobbly serving cart, while endless redundant humiliating ethnic jokes are made at their expense. They will give their back to the smiters, bear our griefs and sorrows, and their food also shall not be consumed.

WHITE JAZZ

The house invention is *La Cuisine Animé,* in which all the fresh ingredients are either moussed or puréed and then reconstructed into the animals from whence they came, an unborn lambkin for example in all its fine gelatinous drag — very *simply* done, of course, but there is another touch, for these animals are also denatured and humanized with the lightest of patisserie: Tania the Tarted Turbot, for example, with her fluted peasant skirt and velouté galoshes on her prehistoric walking fins, a bow on the tail and a dill sprig parasol to keep her mascara from running.

Maestro Luncheon will be released from the androgyny of the corporate buffet, relieved of his pointy shoes and velour sport coats, and armed with pastry guns and skewers of forcemeats will build a crenelated wall of transparent prosciutto, with battlements of béchamel and snow peas, flying buttresses of green snap beans and Louisville lime pie. Bite-sized figures of vanilla extract and allspice will carry veal rolls on their shoulders; a cornstarch and watermelon rind Jehovah will explode from a macaroon sun upon a scene where a marzipan boy is crushed beneath a cart laden with lingonberries. The bulls drawing the cart are of striped sea bass, their craven aspic drivers prodding them with gaffs of celery stuffed with red caviar. The onlooking Evangelists are of tamale and rhubarb respectively, both cloaked in artichoke; the cruising cupids of apricot mousse. Jehovah holds a miter of banana rhumbé, his coriander eyeballs fixed apprehensively upon his own proscenium, a decorous foliage of sculpted tongue and quatrefoil zucchini, niches in which fey madonnas of guacamole conduct business as usual.

SUNDAY

"This is the most outstanding of my works," Maestro announces. "Let's eat." He himself gourmandizes the raisin eyes of the Evangelists, while Sandy recommends the curried pluvial of our Lord, angels of minced quail, and the roasted pimento Abyss. The only thing modern man really controls are his teeth; neither youth nor age; but only after-dinner dreams of both. We shall feed their images *back* to them, intort, contort, frame by frame, the customers eyeing each other uneasily as Tania's anthropomorphized fishiness is gouged repeatedly with a large spoon, and then suddenly, without warning or ceremony, Wanda will slip our distracted guests a small piece of something perfectly done — a braised chop or grilled fish, say, no more than three bites, and a mote of quiet will parachute over the tables, a swipe at ancient awe.... For is this not the modern way? That such machinations and protestations are a necessary prelude to the obliquest dread reference to love and beauty...the point being that one day, before the strike, before the Feds come in to audit, before the cash flow defibrillates, one day, the probability is excellent that Sandy will see Winnie Tranquilla enter his establishment... that his restaurant will have a reason, his food a season, and his long circuitous and final seduction will have its resolution in sight....

The mob seemed strangely attenuated, depressed even. Sandy counted himself integral to the vast cultural sadness. His emotions were no longer human scale. He cannot return to the maples, mums, and finches; all smoke, shadow, and pain. The fact is that people like growth but not growths. This is the problem of the Third Eye. Sandy feared he might be the only one left holding a balloon, holding the bag that floats on its own. But this much is to be said for Sandy; that he believes no part of life should be lost, and that Winnie alone, no-show or not, loves him for this, his only virtue.

He was staggering slightly. To escape the sun, he retreated to the darkened game room. "Young men not in the system," Haas has said, "are ready for war." And it was true, there was not one woman in that room; a chamber of chaotic improvement and constant trading up. Young men hunched over the machines, hugging them with their thighs, crammed into cockpits, knees in their chin, amidst the deafening sounds of war — the monotone of lasers, whoosh of torpedoes, arias of smart bombs, the entire arsenal of weapons, those obsolete and still on the drawing board, having in common only the inhuman immeasurable delay between the pressing of the button and the actual firing of the mechanism, that inevitable period of dumb summation, about which Haas has warned. The games seem to continue whether they are coined or not. What was going on was a game of the game. The beaming back of Bad Light at itself.

Sandy wanders the arcade awash with broad concussive effects of battle, the ultrasonic screams of feigned dying and simulated rejoicing. The animals are up there all right, right up there on the boards, scurrying about, baring their perfect white teeth. But there is something wrong with the animals. They are a bit abstract these animals, they move voraciously but somewhat stiffly. They have no pretensions about looking human, they have taken off their too tight shorts; they are *nude* animals, all

SUNDAY

rumpled foreskin and purplish labia minora, caught in disintegrating mazes, the extent of their surprise is self-limiting, more grumpy than sassy...they move as if they have been...wounded. Both their revenge and serenity seem to have lost simplicity of purpose.

A dark gentleman, very much like the one on the ARTS Channel, has his face thrust far into the cowling of a machine, his pelvis rocking her silly. "¡Mágica!" he is yelling. "¡Destino! ¡Libertad! ¡Muerte! ¡El Sueño! ¡No estoy solo!" But the new machines are on phlegmatic pilot; they do not tilt.

Sandy passes the groups of young men and the names of the games flashing above them; *Thrash the Masterpiece, Shrinking Violet, Mad Man, Persecution, Firebug, Make or Suffer History, Your Faddah's Doop, Your Mudder's Chooch.*

"¡Ah ha," mutters the protoSpaniard from the cowling, "todo el ingenuo disfraz!"

Those games featuring women and heros have been moved to the rear of the hall along with the obsolescent ball sports, between the passport photos and the soft drinks. There is no one left to feel superior to. But back here, next to an antique "Tell Your Weight and Fortune," Sandy comes upon Haas's failed franchise.

His sensuous quarter starts him down a shimmering gray road. The joy stick is padded and has a short smart throw. Also two firing mechanisms, though the nature of the weaponry is as yet unspecified. This is a stripped down model; there is no speed control. He can only go faster and faster; increase the rate of increase. An animal appears on the right shoulder of the highway, his intentions and genus quite vague. Whatever he is, he still counts one point, one letter in the final word, and a *P* appears above him in digitalese. The controls appear to be quite sensitive; it is easy to make a mistake. Clouds float plasmatically above the road and one encounters occasional squalls, patches of viscous rain. You can survive only by burning forward. Cover your rear and blast a clear path ahead. A cemetery, Christian more than likely, is coming up, but it is on the far side of the road and counts for nothing; he will be spared starting over. The score and initials of the best player of the day appear above him on the board — *The Dreamer* has anticipated him once again — she resides in the 99th percentile.

Another animal, pretty ugly in the face, right in the middle of the road! Sandy swerves expertly, *P R* flashes, and at the same moment an institutional structure looms on the right upon a grassy knoll, church, college, business, factory, or tomb it is impossible to tell, but the word is nevertheless doubled, *P R O O*. He is nearing the fatal ejaculation, he requires a second player, some unabashed competition, when he suddenly comes to grips with the technology of the armature, finds a button that turns the rain into rock, the rock into fused metals, the metals into missiles, the word is held back while the missiles demolecularize the animals, which are now monsters. This is a very valuable technique.

There is of course a caveat. It is that the animals become monsters only in the context of the missiles. They are, in essence, not particularly threatening. Left to their own devices they are rather cute, though cuteness in fact may be the dearest enemy. One must attribute to them evil intentions, must firmly believe in their potentially mean reach. But, as it turns out, the monsters tend to be fairly cooperative in their own destruction. They consciously give the illusion that they are illusory. They advertise their falsity. They forewarn the player that what follows is not true. Perhaps this is why they must be destroyed, why such a lavish redundancy of firepower is provided. Without them, one must admit, the highway with its unmarked cemeteries and ubiquitous nondescript buildings would be superlatively vague. For there seems to be no end to the journey except the score of monsters killed.

The subroutines of life are as follows. They are absolute and should be committed to memory:

The object of the game is to guide the small figure in the vehicle, the capsule and its fluid, along the highway and avoid the monsters you think are trying to kill you. There are two ways to kill monsters. One is to crush them with a rock. But if you forget to move out of the way, you may be crushed as well. Players receive no points for their own deaths. You never know how many points a monster is worth until you wipe him out. This is what gives the game "momentum."

The second way to kill a monster is to inflate him. Pump him up until he explodes on his own. This is the more modern way. Only when monsters are partially inflated is it possible to run right through them. Most monsters are diffident, even shy, and appear for only six seconds.

When a monster is killed, a flower will appear on the top of the screen. This is your way of keeping count. Not all of the monsters have to be killed. You will always be ahead of them if you keep punching. It's not necessary to knock them right out of the country.

A note on technique. Some conservative players will try to stall the monsters: count them rather than kill them. This is the mark of the true intellectual. But if you continue to stall, the word will be completed and you will become a full ghost. Full ghosts are not eligible for bonus games.

The patterns you will develop are largely predictable, but they will have to be modified as the game approaches mature mach speeds. After the 99th round a seasoned player will have developed a number of successful patterns, but then the counter goes back to zero and the flowers you have accumulated will disappear. The only flaw in the system is that it will not register scores beyond 99. At 99 you become lovable and a new configuration, not yet on the market, is required. Your real destination is only beyond. At 99 you will remain in the number-one spot until the owner decides to erase all the scores.

Sandy took all his loose change and put it in the slot. The joy stick sprang back to neutral. He backed off and felt no shame. The honorable thing to do was to let the story go on. In a world of ghosts, two-thirds of a ghost wins.

Back from the wars, overdecorated, Sandy limps to Wanda June, puts an arm about her, cups a breast, and kisses her softly about the ears.

"Wanda June," he lamented, wiping his grin off, "this isn't funny anymore. This is serious."

"I think," she said, batting her wet eyes, "we're about as serious as we're going to get."

A host of cherubim balloons were released from the crowd into a scalp of sky. Somebody exploded one with a cigarette and it emitted a horrific scream.

"Then we've been de-seriousized, somehow," Sandy said.

Wanda June hugged him. Sandy's entire space was slack.

"Maybe it would do you good to hit the road for a while, Sandman." She kissed him softly on the shoulder.

"I been there before," Sandy nodded abstractly as the PA system instructed them to move to the westernmost railing for the Special Attraction. "Haas is right. Things will be finished here. And it will be all one thing or the other."

The Conquerors had shifted into a final inchoate medley.

"What is it you want exactly?" Wanda June inquired. "I've never understood."

"I want"...tears appeared in the corners of Sandman's eyes. "All I want," he choked, "...is to be a man...a man ...known for his pleasures."

"Oh, don't give me any of *that* jive, that downer talk, Sandman." Wanda June shook her finger in his face. "We play hard maybe, but we work hard, too. We made it our way, the hard way, and nobody can take it away from us. Why, just look around. Aren't we the freest people ever? We cannot be... *affected.*"

Sandy was about to reply, but he was interrupted by some uncharacteristically formal chords from *The Conquerors,* uncircumstantial pomp, half hymn, half hype.

> *Their sound is gone out,*
> *gone out to all lands*
> *and their words*
> *unto the ends of the world.*

Directly across the expressway the convoy had left the cloverleaf following a bulldozer, backhoe, and mobile crane through a whirlwind of coppery earth. As the green sod was removed, a tortive mist rose up.

All eyes were on the crane as its claw hoisted a burnished preassembled girder system into the westerner's sun. The shadow of the grid, a matrix of elastic rhomboids, spread inexorably across the expressway and enfolded the assembly in its pattern. The construction continued doggedly, jerking and subsiding in little turbinoid fits, to general commotion and applause. But in surprisingly short order the framework of the tower was erect, and in the early incandescent dusk, as gray coils of cement gushed about its base, the unmistakable panels of *Golden Harvest* were unpackaged.

SUNDAY

All powers connected, the sign at the top of the tower was illuminated. It revolved slowly, round and round, until it entered what was once called our point of view

flashing

CIELITO LINDO II

FICTION $7.95

WHITE JAZZ
Charles Newman

WHITE JAZZ is a novel of and for the eighties by one of the acknowledged modern masters of our comically desperate age. Sandy, aka the Sandman, leads a life illuminated by the glowing rays of the computer terminals at the Department of Human Resources, and by the pulsing strobes of the El Cielito Lindo Lounge, disco pleasure palace and source of the ever-changing parade of companions in his non-stop search for satisfaction. WHITE JAZZ is a week in the life of the Sandman, seven days spent lost in the tangled cloverleafs of the World as We Know It, cruising the labyrinth of computer circuitry by day and the chaos of disco humanity by night.

PRAISE FOR NEWMAN'S PREVIOUS BOOKS:

For *New Axis:*
"One of the best American...novels since *The Catcher in the Rye*... *New Axis* taxes the vocabulary of praise." —*Life* magazine

"The world has a major new novelist." —Detroit *News*

For *The Promisekeeper:*
"These works...establish Newman as one of our most exciting and unpredictable writers, one with an amazing range of styles and worlds." —Joyce Carol Oates, *Partisan Review*

For *There Must Be More to Love than Death:*
"Newman has always been a writer's writer, a poet-philosopher who never forgets that poetry and philosophy are pointless except when their concern is with people...The beauty of his prose is the reason his books work." —John Gardner, Washington *Post Book World*

COVER BY DAVID TAMURA
THE DIAL PRESS   0184   ISBN: 0-385-18863-3